Night Shift in Barcelona

Welcome to Santa Aelina University Hospital…

As night falls on Barcelona's busiest hospital, its bustling wards transform… From the hush-filled NICU to the tense operating room, the Spanish city might be fast asleep, but St. Aelina's night shift team are *always* on standby for their patients—and each other! And in the heat of the Mediterranean night, that mix of drama and dedication might hand the hardworking staff a chance at summer love!

Set your alarm and join the night shift with…

The Night They Never Forgot by Scarlet Wilson

Their Barcelona Baby Bombshell by Traci Douglass

Their Marriage Worth Fighting For by Louisa Heaton

From Wedding Guest to Bride? by Tina Beckett

THE NIGHT THEY NEVER FORGOT

SCARLET WILSON

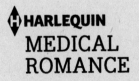

HARLEQUIN

MEDICAL
ROMANCE

Special thanks and acknowledgement are given to Scarlet Wilson for her contribution to the Night Shift in Barcelona miniseries.

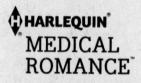

Recycling programs for this product may not exist in your area.

ISBN-13: 978-1-335-73720-5

The Night They Never Forgot

Harlequin Enterprises ULC
22 Adelaide St. West, 41st Floor
Toronto, Ontario M5H 4E3, Canada
www.Harlequin.com

Printed in U.S.A.

Scarlet Wilson wrote her first story aged eight and has never stopped. She's worked in the health service for twenty years, having trained as a nurse and a health visitor. Scarlet now works in public health and lives on the West Coast of Scotland with her fiancé and their two sons. Writing medical romances and contemporary romances is a dream come true for her.

Books by Scarlet Wilson

Harlequin Medical Romance

Neonatal Nurses
Neonatal Doc on Her Doorstep

The Christmas Project
A Festive Fling in Stockholm

Double Miracle at St. Nicolino's Hospital
Reawakened by the Italian Surgeon

Changing Shifts
Family for the Children's Doc

His Blind Date Bride
Marriage Miracle in Emergency

Visit the Author Profile page
at Harlequin.com for more titles.

To my fellow authors Tina Beckett, Louisa Heaton and Traci Douglass, thanks for making this continuity an easy journey!

**Praise for
Scarlet Wilson**

"Charming and oh so passionate, *Cinderella and the Surgeon* was everything I love about Harlequin Medicals. Author Scarlet Wilson created a flowing story rich with flawed but likable characters and… will be sure to delight readers and have them sighing happily with that sweet ending."
—*Harlequin Junkie*

**Scarlet Wilson won the 2017 RoNA Rose Award
for her book
*Christmas in the Boss's Castle***

CHAPTER ONE

CAITLIN MCKENZIE'S HEART skipped more than a few beats as she ran up the last couple of stairs and threw open the doors to the helipad on the roof of St Aelina's. Against a too-dark night sky the glittering lights of Barcelona twinkled around her. The wind caught her hair instantly, her ponytail flapping around and several strands escaping against the warm breeze of the May night.

Usually, she loved this view. Few people knew that this was her escape. When things got too much in Theatre, when the stresses and strains of the job threatened to crack her strong veneer, Caitlin always escaped to the roof of the Santa Aelina University Hospital in Barcelona. From here she could gaze over the city, marvel at the outline of the Sagrada Família, raise her eyes towards Montjuïc Castle or turn and look out across the ocean and sometimes dream of back home in Scotland, where, doubtless, the temperature would be much colder.

No one would really believe her, but the similarities between Glasgow and Barcelona were not lost on her. Both were vibrant cities, full of colourful characters, multinational residents, fabulous restaurants and bars and a complete zest for life that she found hard to capture with words.

Barcelona had welcomed this Scottish girl like a warm hug and she'd be grateful for ever. It had taken her a few years to find her feet. She'd mastered the language, and her specialist role within the hospital as a cardiothoracic surgeon meant she could take referrals from all across Spain.

Just like this one.

She licked her dry lips and clenched her hands into fists as she watched the flashing lights of the approaching helicopter.

She couldn't believe she was about to set eyes on a link to Javier Torres again. It had been twelve long years. Her skin prickled, and it wasn't the stiff breeze from the incoming helicopter.

It was the memory of waking up next to

those dark brown eyes and that warm-skinned too-handsome-for-words guy. Her stomach plummeted. They'd been rivals all through their time together at medical school in London, constantly pushing each other in the pursuit of one triumphing over the other. It had been relentless but strangely helpful. Caitlin had never stopped working hard. The thought of someone nipping at her heels for the best placements, the best opportunities had kept her at the top of her game. She'd spent her life at home keeping her head down and staying out of the firing line of her argumentative parents, who'd barely noticed she was there and never encouraged her. Attracting the attention of the good-looking, articulate Spanish young man had seemed odd to Caitlin. But he'd been straight with her right from the start. 'I'm keeping my eye on you. Apart from me, you're the brightest in the class. I need to make sure you stay beside me and not ahead of me,' he'd teased within a few days of meeting, and then for the next six years.

It was safe to say that at times Javier Torres had driven her completely crazy, challenging her, questioning her, teasing her and occasionally fighting with her. They'd even had a few stand-up rows, much to the amusement of the rest of their class. But he'd always respected her, and she him. At every exam time she'd checked her own marks first, then Javier's second. He was the only person who'd rivalled her.

The night they'd spent together when they'd graduated had been the result of years of pent-up attraction, relief, exhilaration and exhaustion, coupled with a few bottles of expensive champagne. It was a night that she would never, ever forget—the look in his eyes, the feel of his skin next to hers, the lack of inhibitions and the overwhelming sensations of finally connecting with her perfect rival. But as the sun emerged after hours of connection the glow she'd felt earlier had seemed to vanish. The confused emotions and awkwardness of the next morning had sat like a cold, heavy lump in her chest ever since. And if Caitlin could go back and do that morning over, she would. It might not change the eventual outcome of hurried goodbyes and the immediate loss of their momentary closeness, but at least she would have tried.

And at least then she might not still be nursing a broken heart.

How dramatic.

She shook her head at herself as the heli-copter moved in to land. This wasn't about her. This wasn't about him. This was about the fact that the patient she'd agreed to see, assess and potentially operate on was Javier's sister, Natalia.

The request hadn't come from Javier. It had come from the Condesa de Maravilla, Javier and Natalia's mother. That might have stung a little—that Javier hadn't asked himself—but Caitlin didn't know how much Javier was involved in his sister's care.

There was an obvious conflict of inter-est. As a fellow cardiothoracic surgeon, Ja-vier couldn't possibly operate on, or treat, his own sister. Part of her wondered if he'd rec-ommended her to his mother…but that might be pushing things too far.

She'd always known that coming to live and work in his homeland, and both working in the same specialty field, it was likely their paths would cross at some point.

They'd had mutual patients. Their personal assistants often referred patients between them, on their behalf. But Spain was central to most of Europe so referrals also came from other sources. Caitlin's reputation for excel-lence, alongside a newly developed procedure within valve surgery, had meant that her surgical skills were greatly admired.

She was proud of herself. Growing up in a small flat in Glasgow, with a mum and dad who'd dropped in and out of her life, meant that Caitlin had worked hard, securing a scholarship to land her place at medical school at London. Most of her school friends had been surprised at her choice. University fees were paid in Scotland. She had easily achieved the grades to meet the requirements for any of the Scottish medical schools. But, instead, she'd chosen to study in England, where fees were higher and not completely covered for those from Scotland. But Caitlin had been determined. The medical school in London was linked with a prestigious hospital where cardiothoracic surgery excelled. She'd known from an early age where she wanted her career to go, and training in that medical school meant that Caitlin had met all the right people, learned from the best and made many contacts that would help her excel in her career.

She'd had to sign a contract to say she wouldn't take a part-time job during her studies. The university wanted their students to spend all their time studying. But her scholarship had only covered her fees, books and boarding. Caitlin had still needed to eat. So, when Javier had come into the bookshop and discovered her secret Caitlin had been distraught. Her biggest rival now had a chance to get her expelled from school.

She'd been worried sick as he'd pasted a smile on his face and walked across the bookstore towards her. 'Looks like you're working?' he'd said.

It was his casual stance. Those dark, knowing eyes. The teasing glare.

'I have to eat,' was all she could say as she'd grabbed the biggest stack of books she could and walked in the other direction.

He'd followed her around the quiet shop as she'd slotted them onto the shelves. 'Is this where you've been going after class? I thought you were taking extra lessons—or studying.'

'I study in the early hours of the morning,' she'd snapped. 'There's not enough hours in the day to do everything I need to.' She narrowed her gaze and stared hard at him. 'Not all of us are dripping with gold.'

Javier had looked momentarily stunned. Then he'd leaned back and looked at her again.

'Are you going to report me?' she'd snapped.

His answer was instantaneous. 'Why would I do that?' Before she had a chance to say anything, he'd continued in an almost offhand way, 'If I get you kicked out, how will I prove that *I'm* the better surgeon?' He'd raised his eyebrows and turned and walked out of the door, while her stomach turned over and over.

And that was it. Javier had been as good as his word. He'd told no one about Caitlin's job, and even made a few excuses for her when she'd missed non-compulsory labs due to shifts. And his assistance meant that Caitlin was able to study and work in order to keep her place at the medical school of her dreams.

She would always feel as if she owed him for that. And that made it rankle even more.

Her hair was tossing in the wind like crazy; with each auburn strand she pulled away from her vision, another one instantly replaced it. Her ponytail band was no match for the fierce force from the helicopter rotor blades as the vehicle glided to a halt on the landing pad.

A few particles of dust hit her eyes and she averted her head as she rubbed them, still taking steps towards the body of the helicopter. The irony was she could do this with her eyes closed. She'd met many choppers, in countless emergency situations, and the only difference this evening was the patient.

A warm hand landed on her shoulder. 'Okay, doc?'

Marco, one of the cardiac technicians, was beside her. She nodded and blinked a few times, until the particles of dust finally freed themselves from her eyes. Her actions were automatic now and she reached the door of the helicopter in seconds, her arm thrusting the sliding door back with force.

A female voice started speaking instantly. It was the doctor doing the transfer—a serious-looking woman in her mid-forties, with her hair pulled back in a slick bun. This woman was used to helicopter travel. She kept talking, relaying medical details while pushing the end of the mobile stretcher towards Caitlin. The legs with wheels automatically extended to the ground as she pulled the stretcher closer, her on one side and Marco on the other. Another member of Caitlin's team appeared from the side, grabbing the portable monitor and oxygen cylinder attached to the patient and clipping them into place on the stretcher. The doctor kept talking, giving all transfer information for her patient, reporting heart rate, blood pressure, oxygen saturation and the results of her latest X-ray.

Amongst the noise, the wind and the dark, Caitlin's focus was unwavering, her eyes fixed on her patient—Natalia Torres. Her long dark hair, usually lustrous, was limp and damp and her Spanish skin was paler than usual. But her dark eyes were bright and interested and her hand clasped Caitlin's instantly. *'Hola, mi amiga,'* she said, a smile painted on her face.

Caitlin bent down and kissed Natalia's cheek, returning her greeting in Spanish. She'd known Natalia ever since she'd met Javier eighteen years earlier. She'd even spent a few holidays at the grand ancestral family estate in Spain and got to know Javier's sister a little better. They'd remained in touch, meeting for lunch or dinner a few times a year, if both were available to catch up. Their friendship had vexed Javier, Natalia respecting the woman who challenged her brother and Javier sighing that 'now he had to deal with his sister being best friends with his rival'. But the subject of Javier rarely came up between the two women. It was clear that Natalia realised something had once happened between them, but she was too classy to ask questions and for that Caitlin had always been grateful.

The doctor jumped down from the helicopter and Caitlin started to walk alongside the stretcher, just like she always did, to get her patient down to the fourth-floor cardiology unit as soon as possible, but something stopped her.

She couldn't even say what it was. It was like a charge. A lightning bolt in the sky that only she could see.

The helicopter blades had slowed but hadn't quite stopped yet. But she could sense someone else on the roof with her.

She was conscious of her thin, pale pink scrubs, hugging every curve of her body, and the continual unruly behaviour of her untamed hair. As she turned around, she tugged her ponytail band from her hair, and froze.

The black and gold scrunchie dropped from her hand.

Javier. Javier had emerged from the pilot's seat of the helicopter. Javier was the pilot? She hadn't even looked at the person in the pilot's seat—the dust had distracted her and she'd never for a second imagined it might be someone that she knew.

She couldn't move. His brown eyes were

locked onto hers. So much recognition, so much depth—so much more. She drank in everything about him in an instant. White shirt, dark trousers, short dark jacket. For all intents and purposes, it could have looked like a regular pilot's uniform. But nothing about Javier Torres was regular. Not the way his broad shoulders filled out the jacket, nor the way the white shirt revealed the planes of his chest or how the dark trousers rippled against his muscular thighs in the wind.

At university they'd both been runners, pounding the paths and tracks at ridiculous times of the day and night—conscious of the fact a healthy body and mind contributed to cardiovascular health. It was clear that Javier, like her, was still a runner.

All of this taken in, in a blink of an eye.

And whilst Caitlin took in all of Javier's familiar form, her eyes were fixed on his face. She could see something else in his dark eyes—worry. Of course, he was here with his sister. Natalia's surgery would be complicated and had to be carefully planned. Caitlin had scheduled a full two weeks of preparation time to allow her to assess Natalia fully, and be sure about how to proceed. As a fellow surgeon he understood the risks in a way that most people didn't.

She should feel embarrassed. Last time she'd seen Javier he'd been naked, and so had she. In her head she'd always imagined she'd meet him again one day, probably at a conference with their cardiac contemporaries. In those daydreams of course she'd be in a sharp suit, with razor heels, perfect make-up and her auburn hair straightened and tamed. In every way she'd hoped she would look perfect—perfect enough that Javier might have paused to wonder what might have happened between them. She would have oozed confidence and sophistication. She would be polished and presenting at the conference, with everyone in awe at her expertise. Yes, those dreamlike imaginations generally occurred late at night, after a glass of wine, while she was curled up in her pyjamas. But a girl could dream—couldn't she?

Javier blinked. That single tiny action brought her back to the real world. One of the edges of his lips was turned upwards. Was he amused that she'd been frozen in space and time, staring at him with the whole of her life and regrets likely on display across her face?

A swift blast of cold air made her body

react. She ran to catch up with the stretcher, catching more of the report from the staff doing the transfer.

Her brain was full. She needed to concentrate on her patient, not the man on the roof. It was ridiculous. Of course he would want to monitor his sister's condition.

But the shock of seeing him again meant her body was reacting in a way she hadn't expected. Her skin was tingling. Her whole skin. As if an army of centipedes were marching in formation over every single cell. It was affecting her focus and concentration, sparking off a million memories she normally kept locked tight inside.

One of his fingers tracing down the length of her spine as they'd lain tangled together. His mouth nuzzling at the base of her neck. The brush of his jaw with his overnight growth scratching the skin on her cheek. All things that had been imprinted in her brain for the last twelve years and refused to move.

Part of her brain still couldn't really understand how it had all happened. Their fellow students had always called them the 'frenemies'. And they'd been right. She'd just never imagined that so much had bubbled beneath the surface between them, just waiting to erupt. And when it had…

It wasn't that she'd lived the life of a nun after her night with Javier. She'd dated, had a few short-term relationships, then a longer-term disaster. Trouble was, in the back of her mind, none of them had ever lived up to what she'd experienced and shared with Javier.

Sometimes she wondered if she'd romanticised that night. Remembered too much with affection that hadn't actually been there. But she hadn't mistaken the awkwardness between the two of them the next morning. That horrible feeling was also imprinted on her brain, in a way she'd always wanted to erase.

She'd instantly been defensive. Desperate to not lose face in front of her rival. She'd said the first words she'd thought of, turning their night of passion into something so much less. 'Well, at least we got that out of our system,' she'd tried to joke. 'Now we can go back to doing what we do best—fighting for the best roles and opportunities.'

His face had been unreadable. But he'd murmured something in agreement and she'd pretended that her heart hadn't plummeted straight down to her very bare feet as she'd scrabbled to find her clothes. That moment had stayed with her for far too long.

The way the edges of his lips had just turned up flashed back into her mind. Why was Javier here? To toy with her? They'd had virtually no contact for twelve years. That didn't make sense. Or maybe, like herself, he'd just had a flashback to that night.

That would give her a bit more comfort. To know that the night she'd never forgotten was imprinted in his brain, just as much as it was in hers. But after twelve years, it was unlikely.

Javier had always liked to surprise her. She should have expected this. It used to be that she'd known this man like the back of her own hand. Twelve years couldn't have changed him that much, surely?

The elevator doors slid closed behind her, sealing her into an instantly quiet and wind-free space and leaving Javier behind for now. The ability to hear properly again made her ears pop. As the elevator started its smooth descent, she glanced at the monitor to watch Natalia's heart tracing. For someone like Caitlin, the PQRST wave of the heartrate told her just as much as a carefully written instruction manual.

The doors opened again to the bright white straight lines of the state-of-the-art cardiac unit. Caitlin knew how lucky she was to work here. In Spain, there were two cardiac units that everyone held in esteem. One was here, St Aelina's in the middle of Barcelona, the second was in Madrid, the unit that Javier worked in.

They'd always tried to impress each other before. He'd clearly heard about her heart valve research. But she was quite sure that Javier was doing cardiac research of his own. Him being here was unsettling. How much was he going to be around?

She gave a little shiver as the shock of seeing him again caught up with her. She glanced down as she clamped her hands onto the rail of the stretcher and pushed it along the corridor to the already organised private room.

'Okay?' Marco was looking at her from the other side of the stretcher. The experienced older cardiac technician missed nothing.

Caitlin glanced down at her pale pink scrubs again, grimacing at her appearance as she gave Marco a quick nod. She tugged back her hair, feeling in her pockets for another scrunchie to no avail. At this rate she'd end up with an elastic band in her hair and it wouldn't be the first time. Her make-up had likely slipped from her face around six hours ago. She wouldn't know; she hadn't had a chance to consider her appearance since she'd got showered and dressed at six this morning. Even her multicoloured flat shoes that were her trademark at work didn't amuse her. It didn't matter that she had around ten different pairs, and they were as comfortable as slippers. Her whole appearance was about as far away from the message she'd wanted to convey to Javier Torres the next time she saw him as it could possibly be.

Too late now.

She put a wide smile on her face and touched Natalia's arm as the stretcher slid into the room. It was the largest on the fourth floor. All centralised monitoring was installed and a wide internal window gave a clear view of the nurses' station but could be shaded if required. There was an accompanying easily accessible bathroom and, whilst this was still a hospital, the Condesa had already organised a private chef and a team of private nurses to assist with Natalia's care.

It had already been a bit of a battle. Caitlin had high standards for any staff that she worked with; she'd had to approve the nursing staff, to make sure they were suitably qualified for the tricky intensive care work they would have to undertake. She needed to trust the staff, and she'd made sure that the team of nurses had done all the training they required.

Caitlin gave out her standard list of instructions. New ECGs, a cardiac echo, another chest X-ray. A whole host of blood tests and a few other specialised tests that could only be performed within her unit, by her team. She liked to be thorough.

In the bright light, Natalia looked even paler. For a woman with a normally warm complexion, the effect was stark. Caitlin finished her instructions and gave a nod to the rest of the team as they moved Natalia seamlessly over to her more comfortable hospital bed and got her settled.

Caitlin concentrated on her patient. Natalia's condition was serious. She needed surgery—there was no doubt about that. The latest tests would put the final pieces into the jigsaw puzzle of exactly how delicate the surgery would need to be and, more importantly, the chance of success. Caitlin was nervous. She'd thought hard before accepting the referral. She knew Natalia and considered her a friend. But Natalia wasn't a member of her family, or Caitlin's best friend in the whole world. She knew she could treat her appropriately, and not let boundaries blur. She also knew she was the best doctor in Spain for this particular issue. It didn't make sense to send her anywhere else. So, even though they'd known each other for a number of years, she was certain she was the best person to treat Natalia.

'I'm glad you got here safely. How was the helicopter trip?' she asked.

Natalia smiled. 'With my brother as the pilot I wouldn't dare say anything other than it was very smooth.'

Caitlin tried to suppress all the questions she really wanted to ask about how and why Javier had landed on the roof of St Aelina's.

'What can I do to make you more comfortable?'

Natalia blinked her clearly tired eyes. 'Keep my brother busy. You know what he's like. He'll fret over every detail. I really appreciate you agreeing to be my surgeon. You're probably the only person who can keep him in check. Anyone else he would likely hound to death with questions.'

Caitlin wasn't quite sure how she was supposed to keep Javier busy. Her mind flew to a place it definitely shouldn't go and she could feel her face flush at the thought. There was no way she could let thoughts like that invade her brain. She had no idea what Javier's relationship status was. For all she knew he could be married. Whilst she knew he was a fellow surgeon who worked in Madrid, she'd made a point of never making any enquiries about his private life. She'd decided long ago it was better not to know. She didn't want a life full of regrets. But Natalia's words made her curious. Was there something else going on she didn't know about?

She spent some more time talking to Natalia, leaving the subject of Javier and getting a better overview of the condition that was beginning to affect Natalia's daily functioning. It was definitely time to intervene. She finally left when the personal chef appeared with a light supper for Natalia. She had other patients to review, and tests results to read.

Caitlin made her way to her office at the end of the cardiac floor. She was lucky; it was set on the corner, with two wide windows overlooking the city. Her own apartment didn't have the same views, but since she spent more time in her office than her apartment it didn't really matter. She had a comfortable fold-down sofa in her office, as well as a built-in cupboard where she stored some spare clothes and toiletries, and an en-suite bathroom with shower.

She opened the cupboard and glanced at the mixture of clothing in there. Some professional jackets, skirts and blouses. A few dresses. Some yoga pants, more scrubs, running gear, a pair of jeans and some casual tops.

Nothing wowsome. Nothing that might have the effect she might want.

For a few moments she stared out across the dark, twinkling city and cursed herself. Why was she even letting her brain go there? For all she knew, Javier had taken off in his helicopter again and was halfway back to wherever he'd come from. The chance of the big impact she'd wanted to have after all these years was gone. Instead of smart, sophisticated perfection, he'd got crumpled scrubs, unruly hair and multicoloured flats.

She sighed and sat down, flicking her computer on and starting on a new email. As soon as she started concentrating, all thoughts went to her patients. The part of her brain that focused on Javier would have to wait.

An hour later a smell drifted towards her

room. Caitlin rubbed her nose, wondering if she was imagining things. A few moments later, a shadow appeared on the floor. She looked up. Javier was standing in her doorway, a plate in his hands.

It appeared that he hadn't left after all.

He'd known this would happen—the fact that his tongue would be tied just being in Caitlin's presence again.

One glance at her on the rooftop after twelve long years had literally taken his breath away.

'I bring gifts,' he said, a slight awkwardness to his words that made him want to cringe. Twelve years since he'd last seen her. The girl who'd been his best rival and, even though she didn't know it, his best friend. The girl who'd stolen his heart. The proud, independent, feisty Scottish girl who'd slipped into his life at medical school and he never should have let her slip back out.

Twenty-three-year-old Javier had been an absolute fool.

That first glance of her waiting on the hospital helipad with her auburn hair flapping madly in the wind had made his heart flap in a similar manner. Now she was here. In her office. The place she'd fought for, worked hard for and rightly won. He couldn't be prouder—though, of course, he'd never tell her. Then she might feel victorious, and Caitlin was *unbearable* when she was feeling victorious. He almost smiled at the thought.

She blinked and stood up. 'Hi,' was all that seemed to form on her lips.

Maybe her brain was as confused as his was right now. It would be nice to think that, but did he really want her confused over a night from long ago when he needed her at the top of her game to operate on his sister?

He paused then took a few hesitant steps inside her office, hoping he would keep his normal confident disguise in place.

He held out the plate. 'I asked our chef to make your favourites, as a thank you.'

She crossed the room and looked down at the plate. He hoped the white chocolate and raspberry muffins were assaulting her senses in all the right ways. It was a poor attempt at bribery, but he'd try any measure.

'I'm surprised you remember,' she said softly.

He felt a pang in his heart. Had she honestly thought he would forget the little details of her that were embedded in him? His reply was soft too. 'Why would I forget?'

Her body gave the tiniest shiver. There was unintended weight to those words that she hadn't expected. And he knew immediately she wasn't ready for this. Not now. Not here. She had patients to concentrate on.

She lifted her eyes and stared at him for a moment. He had no idea what was going on behind those green eyes of hers as they looked up and down the length of his body in a way that made him feel as if she were undressing him. But her voice was light-hearted when she said, 'New job, Javier—flying private charters? Hope it pays well.'

She was joking with him. Something they'd used to do on a regular basis. He had the oddest sensation of coming home. He glanced down at his attire and held out his hands. 'Didn't realise it looked like a uniform. Wasn't thinking when I got ready. Guess I'm just trying to be a regular guy.' He tried to hide his smile.

'Does a Count get to be a regular guy?'

This was how it used to be. At medical school hardly anyone had known he was from a wealthy aristocratic family. But Caitlin had known. And had never once tried to use it to her advantage. In fact, it had the opposite effect on her and on the few occasions he'd offered to help her out financially when he'd known she was struggling she'd point blank refused. She had far too much pride to ever ask for help.

He rolled his eyes and nodded at the muffins. 'Sure, a regular guy with a private chef. When my sister's health is at stake, bribery is allowed, you know.'

She met his gaze. There was so much there. Twelve lost years between them. She lifted a muffin from the plate and walked around her desk, gesturing to the seat at the other side as she moved to flick some switches on her coffee machine.

He could sense she was trying to decide how to play this. He'd turned up unexpectedly. They'd had literally no contact since that last awkward morning after graduation. He'd replayed that day over and over in his head so many times. It had seemed clear that Caitlin had thought they'd made a mistake; she'd made a quick comment—'at least we got that out of our system'—and that they could get back to being rivals again. He hadn't said a word. Hadn't told her how much that cheapened what had happened between them and how, after one taste of Caitlin, she would *never* be out of his system. He'd let the hurt feelings go; he'd wanted to respect her wishes. The embarrassing retreat and hasty exit he'd had to make had been imprinted in his soul. He'd lost the person he'd been closest to for six years. It shouldn't have been worth it. Not for one night.

But, strangely, that night had meant everything. And he was still glad they had gone there. Even if the next morning had been a disaster.

He couldn't help it. His eyes went to her left hand. No ring. The sense of relief was unexpectedly overwhelming.

Ridiculous. And he knew that. He also knew he couldn't take a lack of ring to mean anything at all. Caitlin might well be married and just not want to wear a ring—she was a surgeon after all. She could also be in a long-term relationship. But he couldn't help but hope not...no matter how shallow that might make him.

He swept his arm around the room. 'Corner office? They must like you.'

'Of course they do. I'm their shining star.'

It was the way she said those words. The confidence in herself that had brought him here.

He glanced out at the dark view of the beautiful city of Barcelona, with all the familiar structures easy to pick out.

'You've done really well for yourself.' He said the words with a hint of pride. When any other physician mentioned Caitlin he always said that they'd trained together, and that she was a fine surgeon.

'I like to think so.' Her gaze narrowed slightly. She was getting suspicious of the small talk.

'We should catch up?'

Her eyebrows raised.

'I mean, twelve years is a long time. You could be married, divorced, a mother of ten.'

Her eyes widened. She clearly hadn't expected this line of questioning. 'None of the above,' she said quickly. She pointed to the small array of figures from a popular sci-fi movie. 'Can't you see, I have an empire to take care of.'

He laughed and leaned forward. 'You still collect these?' He couldn't believe it. Caitlin had always been a sci-fi fan. He used to laugh at her joy at finding the then thirty-year-old figures. It seemed her passion was still there.

He couldn't pretend there wasn't a wave of relief that she wasn't happily married. Maybe that was selfish. He was working on the assumption there wasn't a significant other, because surely that would have been her opportunity to mention it.

'What are you doing here, Javier?' Caitlin asked as she put some cups under the machine. It gurgled quietly, brewing coffee and steaming milk in small streams into the cups.

He gave a gentle laugh, trying to keep things simple. 'What do you think I'm doing here? I'm here to make sure my sister's treatment goes well.'

She raised one eyebrow and he realised how that had sounded and lifted one hand in acknowledgement.

He sighed. 'It was a last-minute plan. Natalia's condition has deteriorated quicker than expected. As you know, there aren't many cardiothoracic surgeons, so it made sense for me to assist in the transfer. I didn't want to hire an outside firm—we're trying to keep our presence here a secret to avoid any media interest. I want to be here during her surgery, and after, to make sure everything goes

smoothly. But don't worry; I won't be idle.
I've asked if I can work night shifts on a temporary basis at St Aelina's.'

She looked as if he'd stung her. 'Who did
you ask?'

'Your director, Louisa Gerard. She was
happy for the offer; apparently you have one
colleague on maternity leave and another with
long-term sick issues.' He gave her a worried
smile. 'Don't worry. She's told me I have to
defer to you as the Head of Department.'

She didn't seem to be taking this news well.
Maybe, after twelve years, she still couldn't
bear to have him around. This might be more
awkward than he'd thought. He'd imagined if
she'd accepted the referral to do Natalia's surgery, surely she must have realised he would
want to be close by?

Caitlin carried the coffee cups over and
glanced at her computer and her tense shoulders relaxed slightly. 'Louisa hasn't spoken to
me this evening. But I can see she's sent me
an email. I guess it must be the news about
you.'

'Your mother—' she started, but Javier cut
her off.

'I recommended you to do the surgery.

You're the best. You know you're the best—
well, apart from me.' He gave a short laugh
as he picked up the coffee cup, trying to allay
some of the awkwardness surrounding them.

Caitlin sat down opposite him, peeling the
wrapper from her muffin. She stared him
straight in the eye, her rich Scottish accent
thicker than normal. 'I can see your ego hasn't
changed much.'

He sat up straighter, knowing what might
come next. Caitlin's accent got thicker when
she was annoyed.

'Are you here to check up on me? Don't you
trust me to operate on your sister?' He could
see the indignant feelings breaking through
her careful veneer.

Javier was surprised. 'I wouldn't have told
my mother you were the best if I had any
doubts about you.' He didn't doubt her skills
or competence for a second. She was a rising
star. She'd already had a number of papers
published on the technique she'd developed
around valve surgery. There wasn't a single
other person on the planet he would trust with
his sister's life.

'But I don't need your help,' she said firmly.
'I'll keep you informed of how Natalia does.

You know you can't have anything to do with your sister's care. It's a direct conflict of interest.'

'I know that,' he insisted. 'But is this really so unusual? Most families want to be nearby if a loved one is having major surgery. Why would this be any different?' He was starting to get annoyed. This wasn't going exactly as planned. Then again, there really hadn't been much time to plan. 'I was also told that because of the sick leave and maternity leave you had a waiting list—one they wanted to help bring down by scheduling some night-time surgeries.'

Caitlin blinked. She knew him better than this, and she hated people trying to hoodwink her. It was an expression he'd learned from the many hours he'd spent in her company.

'So, should I expect the Condesa too?'

He shifted uncomfortably in his chair, knowing instantly it was a mistake. That was the problem of knowing someone so well. She knew him just as well as he knew her. She'd know he wasn't being entirely truthful. He gave another sigh. 'No.'

'Why not?'

'My mother is at home, looking after the estate. I'm here because Natalia asked me to come with her. She knew my mother couldn't come.'

Her gaze narrowed. 'This must have been a very short notice decision. Don't you have your own patients to see in Madrid?'

'Yes, of course I do. But I have a team who can cover in my absence. They know I need to be here with my sister.'

Caitlin tilted her head to the side and gave him a strange glance. 'Why is your mother looking after the estate?'

His heart squeezed in his chest and his skin chilled. She didn't know. He'd made an assumption that she might have seen something in the press. Or that Natalia would have told her. But he had no idea how much in touch she'd been with his sister.

He licked his lips and took a sip of his coffee. It didn't help with the dry feeling in his mouth. He raised his head again.

There was something cathartic about this. About seeing the woman he'd remembered in his head for the last twelve years. Her laugh. Her smile. Her accent. The little quirky things about her—how she hated anyone taking the last chocolate biscuit, or how she relentlessly pursued purchasing a certain brand of tea that was only made in Scotland, no matter how ridiculous the delivery costs. Or her insistence on only eating one brand of baked beans. The passion for her patients. The way her brain worked, never switching off, and her endlessly questioning how to improve procedures and care for patients.

He said the words that still hurt. 'My father died unexpectedly three years ago. Natalia has been running the estate since, and doing an excellent job. But I'm worried all the extra stress has exacerbated her condition.' He gave her a sad smile. 'I inherited the title as well as the estate. My parents, and now Natalia, have allowed me the dream of training to be a surgeon. But in the end I'm going to have to go back to take over. My mother is doing the job temporarily. But once Natalia recovers from her surgery I'll take her home and put plans in place to take charge.'

Caitlin sank back in her chair, clearly stunned by his words. Her brow furrowed and she shook her head. 'I am so sorry. I had no idea about your father. I was joking when I called you the Count—just like I always did.'

She was embarrassed by the blunder, and he gave a conciliatory nod. 'It's fine.'

She leaned forward instantly. 'But it's not fine. You can't give up what you do. It's too important. Too many people need your help. Our skills are unique, Javier. We're not instantly replaceable; it takes years to learn what we have.'

'I know that,' he agreed, his heart weighing heavy in his chest. 'And I've been through all this in my head a million times. But I have to put my family first. No one else will.'

She sat stock-still in her chair. He watched as she clearly processed what he'd just told her. He was surprised she hadn't known about his father. There was a pang deep down inside him. Maybe she didn't know the rest of his story either. The prolonged, and then broken, engagement to a family friend—an engagement his mother and father had approved of. But he'd never really loved Herzogin Elisabeth, nor she him. He'd tried his best to love her, to feel anything like the attachment he'd had to Caitlin. Their breakup had been a shock to his parents, and Javier was guilt-ridden in case that had in part impacted on his father's health.

Javier had never really been able to explain things properly. How could he tell his parents that the 'perfect' couple, the man who would be a Count and the woman who was already a Duchess in Germany, the darlings of the press, just didn't love each other? Elisabeth was intelligent, pretty and charming; his parents had adored her. Everywhere they'd gone, photographers had clamoured to take pictures, all asking about the date of the wedding that had never happened.

To the outside world they'd seemed like the fairy tale couple. But Javier knew better. Fairy tales weren't real. He'd tried twice. And failed miserably both times.

In a flash he could picture Caitlin lying next to him in bed, her auburn hair strewn across the pillow, her soft breathing at his neck as he'd stared at the tiny freckles on her nose.

The memory pricked sharply and he stood up just as Caitlin started to speak. 'You know that I'll take good care of your sister, Javier. You can trust me.'

But he'd already turned away. Maybe this hadn't been such a good idea after all. If he worked here for the next few weeks he would likely be flooded with memories of Caitlin. The friend who'd regretted their night together. The one who'd been imprinted on his brain for ever.

As he reached the door the phone started

to ring. He heard Caitlin pick it up. Her voice was steady but he recognised staccato words and knew instantly something was wrong. She replaced the receiver. 'Louisa has cleared you? You can already work here?'

He nodded in response and pulled out the ID badge he'd collected in the last hour.

'Then don't go anywhere, Javier. I'm going to need some help.'

CHAPTER TWO

CAITLIN WENT ONTO automatic pilot. 'Major road traffic accident. Massive chest trauma to at least two patients.' She walked quickly to her wardrobe and pulled out spare blue scrubs, throwing them towards Javier as he stood in the doorway. Luckily his reflexes were as good as ever and he caught them easily. 'Just as well we have a visiting cardio-thoracic surgeon. I can't be in two places at once, so come with me until we assess the damage.' She nodded to her bathroom. 'You can change in there.'

Whatever had been going on inside his head a few moments earlier had clearly been pushed away. He stripped off his jacket and cast it aside on her desk, the top two buttons were undone on his shirt and he pulled it off. She caught a glance of his Mediterranean skin tone and firm abs. He still had it.

In spades. And she had to avert her eyes as he yanked the pale blue top over his head. Before she even had a chance to speak, the shoes were heeled aside, his trousers were off, flung onto her chair, and the scrubs pulled over his muscled thighs.

'Shoes?' he asked.

She opened the cupboard and dug around again, pulling out a pair of white Theatre-style clogs. Size was indiscriminate in these. Just about anyone could wear them. She flung them in his direction and if he objected to the generic shoes distinctly lacking in style he said nothing.

'Let's go,' she said, and he gave her a nod.

'What do you know?'

'Two mid-forties males, driver and passenger in a car that ran a set of red lights and impacted into the side of a building. Both have massive chest trauma. They were five minutes out from that phone call.'

They were walking along the corridor in long strides. Neither of them even contemplated waiting for an elevator, just pushed open the doors and ran down the four flights of stairs to the ER.

She probably should show him around

properly. But Javier was bright enough. He'd figure out where everything was.

The place was in full swing. Caitlin headed straight to the resus room. Javier kept pace with her, glancing from side to side. 'This place is crazy busy,' he murmured.

Caitlin nodded in agreement. 'It is. It just never stops. Barcelona is one of the most visited cities in the world, and sometimes it feels like every traveller takes ill on holiday.' She slowed to read what was recorded on a whiteboard near the nurses' station. 'Here's where you'll find the summary of who is here right now. Four head injuries. Eleven fractures. Six infections. Four with chest pain/MI. Eight for surgical. Twenty-four minor injuries and sixteen paeds waiting to be seen.' She blew a strand of hair out of her eyes. 'We have the same staffing issues as everywhere else. Apparently we've just recruited a fabulous ER nurse from Cuba, don't know his name, just wish he was already here.'

She moved into Resus, where another dark-haired doctor met them. 'Can you meet your ambulances in the bay and assess if you need resus? We have another RTA heading in.' He looked completely stressed and glanced at Javier. Caitlin laid her hand on Javier's arm.

'David, this is Javier Torres, cardiothoracic surgeon from Madrid. Starting work with us for a few weeks, doing nights.'

'Perfect,' sighed David, 'because Julia, your extra on-call doc, is stuck in the traffic jam behind the RTA. At least you'll have an extra pair of hands if you need them.'

Caitlin looked down at her hand on Javier's skin. As David had been talking she'd used all her energy to concentrate on his words because right now the palm of her hand was doing backward flips of recognition of the skin it was touching.

Things like this weren't supposed to happen. A million sensations were shooting through her nerve-endings right now. The heat of his skin next to hers, the feel of the dark hairs of his arms under her palm. So familiar. They might only have had one night together, but they'd built up to that night for more than six years.

Six years of rivalry, teasing and familiarity. They'd regularly sat close together, skin brushing against each other while they'd shared their everyday life. There had been long nights of study, quizzing each other, before falling asleep with heads on the table. There had been multiple hugs for celebrations and tear-filled moments that factored into the job they were training to do. Javier had been the first person she'd told when she'd done her first minor procedure in Theatre as a trainee. They'd fallen asleep next to each other, on sofas, beds at parties, floors, on multiple occasions.

One of the things she'd missed most was being around someone she felt so in tune with, so comfortable with. She'd almost forgotten about the electricity, how somehow the air seemed to spark between them. Every part of that was flooding back with one touch. If she'd thought her skin had gone crazy on the roof, it was nothing to what was happening now.

Javier moved his arm and rubbed it with his other hand. What did that mean? She didn't have time to consider as the screaming alarms of the approaching ambulances echoed towards them. She thrust a package at him with a gown, mask and gloves. Years of practice meant it took them less than ten seconds to be ready.

Javier's long strides towards the ambulance bay meant she had to almost jog to keep up. It was odd. Caitlin was taller than most women but she was still five inches shorter than Javier.

The first ambulance had barely halted before he'd opened the back doors. One of the paramedics jumped out to join them and a nurse from the department appeared at their side.

Caitlin moved around the other side of the stretcher as it was pulled out, looking at the dark-skinned man lying limply, his breath rasping.

'Rian Caballero, forty-two—he was the driver. We think he might have had a MI behind the wheel. The report is he lost consciousness while driving. As he was slumped across the wheel, he's taken more impact on his chest than would normally be expected.'

Caitlin had her stethoscope out instantly, listening. Javier did the same; it was clear they reached the same conclusion. He pressed a button on the machine monitoring Rian's heart and read the strip that came out. 'Looks like an inferior MI, complicated by a suspected pneumothorax on this side.'

Caitlin was impressed by how calm he was. She shouldn't be, of course. She'd been by his side every step of the way in their training. But after spending the last twelve years working with a variety of different personnel it was nice to be alongside someone who never panicked, no matter what the situation.

'I think he has a haemothorax on this side.' She turned to the nurse. 'He needs to go to Resus. Trauma and Cardiology for the MI. We'll assess the next patient.'

The nurse gave a nod and, alongside the paramedic, pulled the trolley inside the department just as the next ambulance pulled up.

This time it was Caitlin who opened the door, and for a split-second paused. This patient had a long thin tube penetrating his chest. The paramedic in the back looked panic-stricken. Her gloves were covered in blood and there were multiple used wound pads lying on the floor of the ambulance.

'We cut and run,' she said bluntly. 'Injury was caused by impact of the car through a shop window that supplies plumbing equipment. He was losing blood so quickly I struggled to get a line in.'

Javier moved to take over, stepping inside the ambulance in a confident manner. 'But well done; you did get the line in.' He glanced at the bag of fluids running and looked down at the patient's chest. Even from her position,

Caitlin knew the pipe had likely directly impacted the heart.

She turned to the staff who had appeared behind her and held up one hand. 'We're going to move this stretcher very, very carefully. Everyone in position.'

She knew she was holding her breath as she gestured for the slow, steady movement of the stretcher, first out of the ambulance and then onto the ground. A path was cleared to Resus, with Caitlin holding the pipe delicately between her fingers to ensure it didn't move and cause any more damage. She was standing on the runner of the stretcher so she didn't have to walk, but she also felt every tiny bump in the journey.

As soon as they were wheeled into Resus a wide-eyed David handed her the transducer for the ultrasound. 'I heard,' was all he said.

It was just what she needed. So, while others attached a blood pressure monitor, cardiac leads and oxygen mask, Javier's hand closed over hers to take over the delicate role of holding the pipe. This time they were both wearing gloves, but she was still conscious of his careful touch.

Her eyes fixed on the screen as the damage emerged quickly. 'Two chambers of the heart affected,' she said, knowing just how serious this was. Javier gave her a signal to go further down that she knew exactly. It was odd how they could communicate without words. She moved the transducer down and gave a nod. 'Also damage to the aorta.'

Their gazes met. This man had a very low chance of survival from injuries like this. His heart was likely to arrest any minute. But the damage to the main blood vessel also meant that he was likely to go into hypovolaemic shock.

Caitlin made the call, even though she knew some would find it controversial. 'Multiple chamber injury, plus major vessel injury. We take him to Theatre and put him on cardiopulmonary bypass to try and increase his chance of survival.'

'Agree.' It was a one-word answer.

She'd expected Javier to argue with her. She'd expected him to ask for more reasoning for this expensive and risky procedure.

If it were possible, her own heart swelled in her chest. 'What emergency theatre is open?' Caitlin shouted, looking around the room.

'Seven,' came the reply. 'Danielle Lunar is the anaesthetist.'

'Tell her we're on our way,' she replied as

she started unplugging the machines around them and piling them onto the trolley.

The other member of the ambulance crew came in with a wallet in his hand. 'Roberto Puente forty-six. Shall I get the police to contact his family?'

Javier replied, 'Please tell them we're going into surgery and will update as soon as we can.'

Caitlin jumped onto the side of the trolley and they moved smoothly and carefully down the corridor to emergency surgery. A few of the theatre staff raised their eyebrows at the sight. Caitlin gave strict instructions and one of the staff took over from her position as Caitlin and Javier scrubbed for Theatre.

All theatres at St Aelina's were well-prepared. A bypass machine was made ready. The anaesthetist pulled up Roberto's details and, even though he was unconscious, she made sure he was anaesthetised and his vitals monitored. What was most surprising for everyone, his heart remained in a slow, galloping kind of sinus rhythm—the normal heart rhythm, even though there were more than a few ectopic beats. If she'd asked a group of students to describe the heartbeat of someone with this kind of penetrating injury she could guarantee not a single one would say sinus rhythm. But it was clear his heart was struggling as the ectopic beats increased.

Once they'd finished scrubbing, Caitlin went to her normal side of the operating table. Javier appeared next to her, then gave a nod and moved to the other side of the table. It was clear, as lead surgeons, they were both used to being on the same side.

'Okay?' she asked before starting.

She always did this. No matter how chaotic a situation, she always asked every member of staff in Theatre if they were okay before she started. It wasn't about being courteous; it was about making sure her team were in the right head space. This would likely be a long shift.

'Good,' Javier said, his dark brown eyes meeting hers. There was no wavering, no doubt, and still no questions about her decision-making. If she could, she would hug him right now.

Somehow, she knew that even though they hadn't been in each other's company for twelve years, Javier would have her back— the way he'd always done. That moved over her like a warm blanket of security. It had been a long time since she'd had that unquestionable comfort.

Her eyes went around all her staff, asking the same question, to answers of assurance.

She looked at her staff member holding the pipe. 'Someone get Lisa a stool, please,' she called.

A stool miraculously appeared and was wheeled in for Lisa to get comfortable on. They wouldn't be pulling the pipe out for a while, and it was important she didn't move.

Finally, when everything was done to her satisfaction, even though it had likely been less than two minutes, she was ready.

'Let's begin,' said Caitlin with confidence as she raised her scalpel.

Javier watched. She was cool, calm and collected. Nothing about Caitlin had changed. Her practice was meticulous. This was why he'd recommended her to his mother. This was why he had confidence that she was the right surgeon to operate on his sister.

Her green eyes were steady. He'd seen the question in them when they'd been in the resus room. She'd made a decision that other surgeons might not have had the balls to make. He would have, and he agreed entirely. But even back in Madrid another surgeon might have asked questions.

Right now, this man had around a twenty per cent survival rate with his catastrophic injuries. He'd just been in the wrong place at the wrong time. His friend had lost consciousness behind the wheel, and by misfortune had driven into a store where the items for sale had caused a penetrating injury to his chest.

The odds of something like this happening were slim. But this was life. And things did happen. And it was up to Caitlin and him to make the big decisions to try and increase Roberto's chance of survival. If he made it out of surgery alive, his survival rate would likely have gone up to around fifty-five per cent. Not great, but a fighting chance.

The surgery was slow and meticulous. The cannulas were put in place for bypass. Bypass commenced, removing the immediate circulating blood from the wound site. The whole theatre held their breath as the pipe was finally removed. Caitlin patched the right ventricle, and Javier patched the left.

The small tear in the aorta was repaired and Danielle kept a careful watch on intravenous fluids and coagulopathy, cardiac rhythm and blood pressure.

It was inevitable that Roberto's blood pressure would reduce at some point in the procedure, but everything else was kept carefully in check. There was always a tricky balance between making sure the blood wouldn't clot too easily and that the patient wouldn't bleed too much during surgery.

By the time Caitlin and Javier had finished their final stitches his muscles and back were starting to ache. He hadn't told Caitlin, but he'd already worked twelve hours before transferring his sister to her care. Now, he'd been awake for nearly twenty-four. No matter how much his senses were on alert around Caitlin, he really did need to get some sleep.

He was impressed by the staff around him. It gave him reassurance for when his sister could be in one of the theatres here. The equipment was all state-of-the-art and the staff well trained and competent.

Roberto was wheeled into Recovery and Caitlin pulled her surgical hat decorated with little hearts from her head. She disposed of her gown, gloves and mask before washing her hands again and walking out into the corridor and finally giving her hair a shake.

'I really should cut this off,' she said.

'Don't you dare.' The answer came out automatically.

She lifted her head and looked at him in surprise. 'Why not?' There was an edge of challenge there. Caitlin had never liked someone else telling her what to do.

'Your hair is gorgeous,' he said without any hesitation. 'I've always loved it.'

She turned towards him. 'But what if I lost it?'

The words still had the same challenge in them. His blood was instantly chilled. Was she telling him she was ill? Because that made him feel sick to his stomach.

Her green eyes were fixed on his. He lifted his chin. 'I'd be sorry to see it go. But if you lose it, you lose it. You're still Caitlin. That won't change.' He gave his best half-hearted shrug. 'I was just commenting that I like your hair.'

He stopped for a moment and put his hands on his hips to stretch out his back. 'Why don't we get some coffee? I need some sleep, but let's eat first.'

She was looking at him in the strangest way. He wasn't quite sure what it meant. But finally she gave a little nod. 'Let me change and grab a cardigan,' she said, ducking into a locker room and emerging with a light cardigan over her changed scrubs. 'I know the best place to go; follow me.'

They emerged out of the hospital main entrance into the early rising sun. Barcelona was framed in a stream of yellow, orange and red. From the dark Sagrada Família outlined beyond and the rest of the city, it was one of the most beautiful sights.

Caitlin sighed. Even though every bone and muscle in her body ached, she could still appreciate the beauty of the city she'd adopted as her own.

'I love this place,' she sighed.

He glanced at her. He'd wondered how she'd settled in his home country. 'You didn't consider the job that came up in London last year?'

'Of course I did.' She gave him a knowing glance. He didn't doubt she realised he'd considered it too. 'But there's something about Barcelona. I love this city. I've found it so welcoming, and the facilities at St Aelina's are second to none. It's my team. Why would I go to London, to be a much smaller cog in virtually the same wheel?'

He nodded, knowing that these were exactly the same thought processes he'd gone through when considering the job in London.

She pointed to a small café across the street. 'Let's go over there.'

'It's open at five a.m.?'

Caitlin nodded. 'It's open twenty-four hours. Let's just say that it learned to cater to the needs of the hospital staff. We do have a staff canteen, which is fine. But this local café has a real captive audience with us straight across the road. You'll love it,' she said with confidence.

She pushed open the door to the old-style diner and slid into one of the booths, giving a chef behind the counter a nod.

He appeared a few moments later with a latte in his hand for her. 'Usual?'

She nodded, and he turned to Javier. 'And what can I get you?'

Javier ordered coffee, an omelette and some toast. He seemed much more relaxed now. In the early-morning sun she could see a few little lines around his eyes. One tiny strand of grey hair at his temple. But there was no doubt about it; Javier was still too handsome for words.

It had always been like this. Anywhere

they'd gone, Javier's tall muscular frame had always caused female heads to turn in admiration. Caitlin had never worried. At first she hadn't thought of Javier in a romantic manner. And when she finally did, she'd realised that Javier had always made her feel like the most important person in the room anyhow and she had nothing to worry about.

'The surgery went well. It was a good call.'

'You don't know how good it is to hear those words,' she said honestly. 'I half expected you to ask questions about it.'

He shook his head firmly. 'I would have made the same decision. It's risky. But the risks of not doing it outweighed taking a chance on the bypass. You've doubled his chance of survival.'

She reached over and touched his hand. '*We've* doubled his chance of survival.'

This time there were no other distractions. This time it was only them, and Javier looked down at her fingers on his hand and put his other hand over hers.

She held her breath. It seemed like such a big moment after twelve years. How was she supposed to interpret this?

Twelve years ago this would have been entirely normal behaviour between them. But that night together had changed everything.

As she looked at those dark eyes her stomach flipped. There was no getting away from it. She was every bit as attracted to Javier now as she had been then. And that broke her heart a little. Because he would never be hers. They didn't move in the same circles. This man was a Count. He had an estate. She came from a council flat in Glasgow—they were at entirely different ends of the spectrum. It didn't matter that he'd never treated her any differently. She knew what the big picture was here. He'd already told her the expectations placed on him now that his father had died. She'd always known this about him, but after they'd slept together and moved in separate directions it had felt as though she'd lost her best friend. That had made everything even sadder for her.

The chef appeared and set down their plates. She glanced down at the scrambled eggs and toast that she always swore by in this place, and knew that her appetite was virtually gone.

Javier looked as tired as she did. 'Do you have some place to stay while you're here?' she asked.

He nodded to his left. 'The hotel just a few doors down.'

Caitlin pressed her lips together. It was an exclusive hotel, with bills to match. Even though it was close to the hospital, it was the kind of place that celebrities stayed when they came to Barcelona—partly because of the spectacular roof terrace and bar that faced over the city. Exactly the kind of place a Count could stay.

As Javier started to eat, Caitlin remembered the plate of muffins that must still be in her office. She hadn't even finished one.

He looked up at her. 'How do you find St Aelina's? I know it's relatively new. Tell me about it.'

She took a breath, wondering if he'd considered the job she'd got there. 'What can I say? It's state-of-the-art. Only a few years old. They've worked really hard to make the building and its surroundings environmentally sound. They also created the park next to the hospital at the same time, and patients and staff are encouraged to enjoy the outdoor space. Solar panels are blended into the design, there is eco-friendly staff accommodation built close to the hospital...' she gestured her head to the left in the direction of his hotel '...which I know won't be as fancy as your hotel but gets good reports. There's a cycle-to-work scheme where staff are given grants to buy bikes, a gym and swimming pool within the hospital, and counselling sessions for staff if required. You'll know that we're a teaching hospital, and I carried out the research for my heart valve work right here.'

'Impressive.' He gave a nod. Was he impressed, or was it just lip service?

She gestured to the right. 'The park is probably one of the best things. There are sculptures from El Poblenou's local artists, a play area for kids, cycle paths and a variety of trails and running paths throughout.'

'That's where you run now?'

She nodded. 'Mainly. I do sometimes pound the pavements of Barcelona, but I don't generally have a running partner, and you know we don't do regular hours. Barcelona, early morning or late night, is the same as every big city—you never know who you might meet. I feel safe running in the park. It's well lit and there are security staff patrolling it on a regular basis.'

He gave a nod and a half-smile and her heart melted a little. This was how she remembered things. The way they'd been so easy around each other.

'How's Madrid?'

He nodded and swallowed the last bit of his omelette. 'Good. I took over from my mentor and have a great team around me, all already trained. It gives me the time and space to do things like this.'

She swallowed, feeling a little envious already.

'It's nowhere near as modern as St Aelina's but I kind of like the traditional. Our theatre space has been redone, and all our equipment is state-of-the-art. We've changed the layout of the unit recently to help with patient flow. But probably the best thing is the new research lab that's been built after acquiring an accompanying building. We have great plans.'

As she watched him, it brought back memories of all the time they'd spent together and how much joy he'd brought into her life. All of it marred by that last night, which had started so wonderfully and ended in a completely confused state.

It had taken her a long time to take a chance on love again. When she finally had, her ex had turned out to be a lying cheat. She'd learned her lesson. When it came to men,

Caitlin now stayed well away and guarded her heart fiercely.

Just sitting here with Javier now made her want to let her defences down. She wanted to reach out and touch him. Feel his skin against hers again, lay her head on his shoulder and feel his arm around her. She wanted it so much it felt like an ache.

'You think your place in Madrid is better than St Aelina's?' She couldn't help asking the question. He'd had a chance to look at her place, but she hadn't seen his. She was curious to know what he thought.

He gave a careful shrug. 'Madrid is familiar. I know that team.' He met her gaze. 'Some trained alongside me, some I've trained myself. I have complete faith in them. Your place...clearly has some staffing issues right now.'

'That's unfair,' she said, automatically defensive. 'All hospitals have staffing issues. Just because I have a staff member who is sick and one on maternity leave doesn't mean we aren't as good.'

'I didn't say that.' But he had an almost smug look on his face. 'It's just that I know most of the staff I have trained will stay. My team are settled. Most of them have families in Madrid. It feels like my team are at the heart of the hospital in Madrid. Barcelona seems a more...' he searched for the word '...transient city.'

He said the words with pride and they rankled. Was this a dig at her, with her lack of family? Or at her because she was happy to leave the place she'd used to call home without many home ties?

She shook her head. The staffing issues were a problem for her. She was sure that was why Louisa had agreed to give him a temporary job. But there was no way she'd admit it to him.

'Our theatres and labs are all brand-new. I'm working alongside one of the medical providers around a surgical tool for vascular surgeries. The prototype is just completed.'

He pressed his lips together and paused before speaking. 'The layout of your unit and theatres is impressive,' he said slowly. 'Our older-style building doesn't lend itself to so much change. Not unless I want the walls to fall down. The work we've currently done is as much as we can do.' He gave a gentle laugh, and she realised he was actually admitting to a shortfall at his place of work, in the quietest of ways.

'I have all the equipment I need. But the idea of further expansion wouldn't work in the heart of Madrid. After acquiring the previous building next to the hospital, we have an embassy on one side and the building of a new motorway on the other.

She wrinkled her nose. 'Noisy?'

He nodded. 'Mainly, it causes more traffic problems right now. Eventually, it should make the traffic around the hospital much smoother.' He rolled his eyes. 'But I sometimes wonder if they'll finish it in my children's lifetime, let alone mine.'

It was like a spear to her heart. 'You have children? I didn't know that.'

He shook his head quickly. 'No. Sorry, just a turn of phrase. What do you call it?'

Her stomach was churning furiously. Why on earth would the thought of Javier having children cause such a visceral reaction in her? It was ridiculous.

He was looking at her with those dark brown eyes. Instantly, flashes of their night together were playing in her mind. Him, tracing his finger down her arm. Sliding his fingers in her hair and resting his hand at the back of her head as he'd pulled her mouth to his.

Caitlin pushed her plate away.

'Something wrong with your food?'

She shook her head. 'I think I'm just over-tired. It was a long day and night. I'm sure I'll feel better once I've slept for a few hours.' She couldn't think straight right now.

He put down his knife and fork. 'Is it just tiredness, or is it something else?'

She furrowed her brow in confusion. 'What do you mean?'

He leaned his head on one hand. 'We should talk.'

Words she would have died to hear twelve years ago.

Now, she was tired, emotional and it all seemed far, far too late.

He'd seen it. He'd seen her face when she'd thought he had children. Her reaction was ridiculous, and completely unjustified. And she didn't even want to explain it to herself, let alone to him. So many unresolved feelings. So many 'what-ifs'.

She shook her head. 'I can't do this.'

'But you know we should.'

That voice. That accent. Like honey on her skin. His deep voice had always sounded like a tune to her.

Her attraction to him was as strong as ever.

'We worked well together in Theatre,' he said. 'I heard one of the nurses refer to us as a dream team.' He gave her a warm smile. 'Isn't that worth talking about too?'

He was right. They had worked today in perfect harmony. No one who'd seen them could deny it. She was trying to push all the current turmoil she was feeling aside. Maybe he hadn't realised what was happening in her head. He looked intense, but cool. When had it got so hard to read Javier Torres?

But a good operating partner wasn't worth the heartbreak she would endure if she started to let her walls be chipped down by the man she'd given her heart to years before.

She had a good life here. A good career. A perfect reputation. She was comfortable. She was happy. So why was she letting herself question that after a few hours in Javier's company?

She couldn't let him upend any of this for her. Already, she was thinking about those flashes of skin in her office as he'd stripped without a second thought. She wanted to see more. One glimpse had been enough for her to lose all her concentration.

She wasn't that person. She was a responsible surgeon.

'It's too late for us to talk, Javier. The time to talk was twelve years ago. And neither of us could manage it. The result was that we both lost our perfect rival. Our sparring partner. I've got no energy to rehash all that with you—and I have no wish to.'

Maybe it sounded blunt. It could be her tiredness was making her lose any sense of tact that she'd once had.

'You don't mean that.' His voice was quiet, with a hint of hurt. For a moment that made her pause.

He pulled a notepad from his pocket and scribbled something on it, pushing it towards her across the table.

'Here's my phone number and my room number. I want to talk, Caitlin. We should talk. Even if it's just to clear the air between us. We're going to have to work together for the next few weeks. I want you to trust me.'

She stared at him, long and hard. 'Trust was never the issue between us, Javier.' She pushed the paper back to him. 'And I'm not going to come to your hotel room.'

He looked at her, clearly hurt, and she realised he hadn't quite meant what she'd thought he had. But it was too late now.

'See you later,' she said as she stood up and

walked over to the counter, leaving money to cover the bill. Then she was out of the door of the café before she changed her mind and risked having her heart broken again.

CHAPTER THREE

TOO MUCH HISTORY. That was what was wrong with them, Javier had decided. He'd only managed to sleep for a few hours, even though the bed was one of most comfortable he'd ever slept on. Thoughts about Caitlin spiralled around in his head, along with his underlying worries about his sister.

He'd realised the hotel room suggestion had come over in the wrong way, but she hadn't given him a chance to explain before walking out and leaving. His pride was a little offended by the fact she'd also paid the bill.

But everything that had happened between them had to be pushed aside. Natalia was the most important person here. He needed to have another conversation with Caitlin to make sure they were on the same page about that, at least.

What good would it do anyhow to pick

apart what happened twelve years ago? He'd have to cast aside the fact it felt as if it had impacted on every other relationship in his life since. Having the person you felt destined to be with slip through your fingers would make any man feel like a fool. Maybe Javier was just a romantic at heart. But, no matter how hard he'd tried with Elisabeth, he couldn't force feelings that just weren't there. She was a nice woman, a good person, and he knew in the end he'd done them both a favour. She'd grown tired of the constant coverage of their relationship in the press; it had put her under intense pressure. So, he'd agreed there would be no announcement about their engagement being off, no declaration. They would both stay silent on the matter to stop any more press intrusion.

Elisabeth had gone on to meet a man she did truly love and had married him recently in secret. Javier was delighted for her, but it still left him nursing a sense of failure.

As he strolled back through the hospital, he was determined to keep all his focus on Natalia.

She was looking tired, but a bit brighter. She was wearing a bright pink nightshirt and her hair had been washed and was pulled back in a ponytail. His eyes went instantly to her monitor to check her readings. Everything seemed in order.

'Heard you were a hero last night, brother,' she said with a grin.

'Who told you?' he asked as he sat down in a large chair in her room.

She waved a hand. 'It's slow at nights up here. But the chat from the night shift staff is good. They were very interested to hear that you were my brother.'

He groaned. 'What on earth did you say to them?'

'Just that you were a cardiothoracic surgeon back in Madrid, and that you and Caitlin trained together.' She gave an amused smile. 'To be honest, I think it was more the old helicopter pilot thing that impressed them. The major surgery was just an add-on.'

'I just checked on that patient. He's doing well. I'm hoping we made the right decision.'

'You always make the right decision, Javier. You know that, and I know that.'

He knew she was getting at other parts of his life. But he didn't want to go down that route right now. Natalia had been key in encouraging him to pursue his career in surgery, while he knew his mother and father had merely tolerated it. Natalia had always wanted to work in the family business, and she'd done it better than he ever could. The conversation about taking his place back at the estate was likely to be met with resistance from her. He hadn't yet told Natalia that he'd had that conversation with his mother.

But he had to think about her health. Natalia's surgery would be risky. There was a chance she wouldn't make a full recovery and her life could remain impacted the way it currently was. She was pale. She was breathless. Her energy was depleted. She tried her best to hide how her malfunctioning heart valve affected her life, but he could see it in her every breath.

She'd accepted the fact she needed surgery. But he was quite sure that neither of them had truly accepted the fact it might not be successful. He hated that he couldn't do it himself.

He wasn't concerned about Caitlin's skills. She was an excellent surgeon. It was that element of lack of control that killed him. There were also the inevitable unknowns that could happen during surgery. They'd happened to him, and every surgeon he'd ever known. His sister could die on the theatre table.

He hated that deep down he knew that if something happened he would likely blame Caitlin. He'd said he was here to help assist her with the waiting list. But it had been twelve long years since they'd worked together. He'd never heard a bad word about her from anyone else, but he wanted to see her work for himself. He wanted to watch her in Theatre. Last night she'd been at the top of her game, but he'd seen that flash of worry in her eyes. And also the look of relief when he'd agreed with her decision-making. Was Caitlin really as confident a surgeon as he thought she was—or did she have doubts about herself? He had to find out. His sister's life depended on it.

'I heard some other news.'

'What kind of news?' he asked.

There was a glint in Natalia's eyes. 'I asked if Caitlin had met anyone lately. Apparently, she's happily single. I thought you might want to know.'

He shifted his feet, not wanting to admit he'd asked the question himself. His sister would jump all over him. 'Why would I want to know that?'

'Because I know you better than you know yourself, brother dear.' She waved a hand. 'I think she's still smarting over the "ratbag" from a few years ago. He cheated on her, and she wasn't so much hurt as livid that she hadn't caught on sooner.'

'How did you know that?'

'We meet, a couple of times a year. It's come up.'

'You never mentioned it.'

She waved a hand. 'We don't normally talk about Caitlin.' She gave a smile. 'And, curiously, she doesn't like to talk about you either.'

She let those words hang there. But Javier didn't want to get into that kind of conversation with his sister. So he went for the most obvious words.

'Fool. He clearly didn't deserve her then.' It came out of his mouth without a second thought.

Natalia shook her head. 'You have no idea how hard it is to try and get information out of you two.'

It was clear she wasn't going to let this go. 'Why are you going on about this?'

Natalia stared hard. 'Because you're a no-go area with Caitlin when it comes to chatting. What happened between you two? You were friends, or maybe friendly rivals is a better description, and then everything just shut down dead. She never asks me a single question about you, and that strikes me as odd. Something must have happened. You trained together for six years. You brought her to the estate a few times so you could both have a break from your studies.'

He gave a shrug. 'You know how she is. You know her circumstances and where she came from. Holidays weren't really an option for Caitlin. It seemed ridiculous that we had all that space, and good weather that we could easily share.'

There was so much missing from that statement. Years ago, he had invited Caitlin to holiday at his estate, twice. She'd initially said no—of course. But once Javier had told her he was flying on a private jet, there would be no costs for Caitlin—because he would still be going home, whether she came or not, she'd finally come around to the idea of taking a week's break from studying. He'd known that part of the issue was not really wanting to go home to her parents in Scotland, but he hadn't pressed her on it.

He'd thought she'd love the huge grounds and vineyards around his ancestral home. But Caitlin had been strangely cold when she'd got there—particularly after he'd told her she could choose from over forty rooms.

It had taken him a long time to realise she must have been overwhelmed by the size, the people and the staff. What had been meant to be a kind offer had maybe looked as though he were pushing his wealth in her face—and that had never been his intention.

Natalia smiled and folded her arms. 'You two are so obvious. There's so much more going on here. But neither of you will spill.' He could see the look of pure amusement on her face.

He folded his arms too. It was a sibling stand-off. 'Well, if she isn't talking, neither am I,' he said, knowing that his sister would never let this go. She had too much time on her hands right now.

'I'll get it out of one of you,' she said, giving him a look of determination. 'I'll find out what happened.'

He shook his head and relaxed back into the chair, preparing himself for the onslaught from his sister.

She kept teasing him, asking about their mutual friends and telling him tales of the staff back home. This was when she was at her most enthusiastic—when she was talking about the job that she loved.

It pained him that there was a chance she might have to give it up. He definitely wasn't ready to have that conversation with his sister. And, knowing Natalia, it would be the hardest in the world. She would fight him tooth and nail for the job that she loved and could do with her eyes closed. But he couldn't let anything impact her health. If this surgery didn't work as he might hope and pray for, then he would have to face the inevitable. His life as a surgeon would be over.

He heard footsteps behind him and turned just in time to see Caitlin walk through the door. She was wearing dark blue scrubs today, and her hair was tied back from her face.

His heart gave an unexpected lurch. His two favourite women in one room. An unspeakable force. It was unlikely he would survive this.

Caitlin gave Javier a sideways glance, then pasted on a courteous smile. Didn't the guy ever sleep? She was hoping he wouldn't be around until the night shift tonight. 'Hi Natalia, hi Javier.' She moved quickly across the room, an electronic touchpad in her hand.

'I'm here to have a chat with you about some of your results.' She asked the question she always asked when family members were present. 'Would you like to discuss this alone?'

Natalia shook her head. 'No. He'll only annoy you later anyhow.' She nudged Caitlin as she sat down at the side of the bed. 'Best to let him think he's involved,' she said with a big grin on her face.

She was smiling, but Caitlin was experienced enough to know that Natalia was slightly worried. It could be that she wanted her brother around for reassurance, and Caitlin couldn't blame Natalia one bit. Her surgery would be serious. For all Caitlin's skill, there was no guarantee that everything would go perfectly. Every patient was different and, in surgery, Caitlin had learned to expect the unexpected and never to take things for granted.

It was time to make some compromises. She could let Javier play a small part in his sister's care. If Natalia needed reassurance, that was fine.

Caitlin turned her electronic tablet to face Natalia. 'Let's have a look at your test results and what they mean. Then I'm going to explain some other tests that we need to do. I'll also explain the procedure to you. I'm going to make a few minor adjustments, based on some of the results I've seen today, but I'll go through all that with you.'

She'd always known it would take up to two weeks to do all the tests she needed. Some surgeons might proceed with the most basic of tests. But some surgeons weren't Caitlin McKenzie. She was more than thorough. She had no intention of going into Theatre and being surprised by anything she hadn't thought of. Some patients found the process of tests exhausting, and Caitlin had made sure to space all of Natalia's tests out. It would also give her time to explain all the results to Natalia and let her process them.

She could sense Javier sitting straighter in his chair, and she could practically read his mind with the number of questions he must want to ask.

Caitlin didn't have brothers or sisters, so she could only imagine how he must feel right now. She turned and gave him a smile of acknowledgement. 'Feel free to ask any questions, Javier, as we go along.'

His face was tighter than normal. He was worried, he was stressed. She could see the shadows under his eyes and wondered if he'd slept at all after their disastrous breakfast in the café across the road.

He didn't say a word, just gave a nod, and for him that was strange.

Caitlin focused her attention on Natalia. She went through the blood tests, the chest X-rays, the cardiac echo and the MRI. Replacement valves were not normally a difficult procedure. But Natalia had some previous scar tissue and some cardiac damage from an infection years ago that had started her heart problems. Her heart was already working harder than it should. It was Caitlin's job to take a long-term approach here. Natalia was only twenty-nine. Quality of life was important. She also had to take into consideration that Natalia might want to have a family at some point. Most women didn't think about it—because they had no reason to—but pregnancy put the heart under considerable strain, as did labour. Caitlin had even taken the trouble to pick up the phone to Natalia's now retired paediatrician; he had first recognised the cardiac infection and Caitlin wanted to be sure she had the full picture before she even lifted a scalpel.

She kept her words factual but tried to be

as supportive as possible in the news she was due to deliver.

Natalia took a deep breath as Caitlin told her the final part of the news. 'So I'll need both a mitral valve and an aortic valve?'

Javier was on his feet, pacing already.

Caitlin nodded. 'Neither of your valves are functioning well. It's putting extra strain on your heart. We'd initially only planned on surgery for the mitral valve. But it's clear we need to replace the aortic valve too. Opening up your chest is a big procedure; the detailed studies we've done have picked things up at an earlier stage. Because of other risks, it's best if we do both surgeries together. I'm still going to run another few tests before I make a final decision.'

Natalia swallowed nervously, and Caitlin handed her the glass of water on the bedside table. 'It's a lot to take in. I'm here for any questions that you have.'

She tried not to look at Javier. His pacing was annoying her, but she knew exactly why he was doing it.

Natalia leaned forward and stared at the screen. She pointed at a few of her results and asked some questions. Caitlin smiled. This was a bright, intelligent woman who'd already considered aspects of her treatment. Being the sibling of a doctor wasn't without its benefits, and Javier and Natalia had clearly had multiple discussions about her care and treatment.

Caitlin did have regrets here. It was clear the news had thrown Natalia as well as Javier. Risks were higher here. The overall statistics on five-year survival for both surgeries were around fifty-five per cent. But age adjustment on those studies meant that someone of Natalia's age had much better odds.

'Sit down, Javier.' Natalia glanced up at her brother but her words were soft. She understood he was concerned. She smiled at Caitlin. 'If only he would spend so much energy on pressing grapes.'

Javier obediently sat and rolled his eyes good-naturedly at his sister. 'If only you would let me near them.'

Natalia laughed and shook her head at Caitlin. 'As if. Let's just say that Javier is much better at operating on people than he is at harvesting grapes.' She lifted her eyebrows. 'Let's just say that takes *real* skill.'

Caitlin laughed too. This was how she remembered them from her holidays at the estate so many years ago. Full of good-natured teasing. It was clear that the siblings loved each other, and she envied that a little. Someone who would always be there to have your back.

She'd never had that. In fact, her relationship with Javier had been one of her few experiences of having someone who had treated her as though she were a priority in their life. His constant niggling at her, competing against her and teasing her had never felt malicious. Sure, it had annoyed her on occasion. But Javier had felt like a steady presence in her student life.

Her mum and dad had both drifted from her life. First with drug and alcohol issues, then with multiple relationships, which inevitably never worked out. It wasn't that she didn't care about them. She did. In a kind of far-off way. Much like the way they obviously felt about her.

As a child and teenager, her neighbour next door had been more of a constant in her life, encouraging her to study, occasionally feeding her breakfast or dinner and helping her apply to university.

When Mary, her neighbour, had taken poorly a few years ago, it was Caitlin who had gone to see her, and looked after her before she'd died. Mary's diagnosis had been very late, but she'd been happy and her pain well controlled. 'I'm so proud of you,' she'd whispered as she'd stroked Caitlin's face. It was Caitlin who'd been holding her hand when she'd taken her last breath and she'd known it was absolutely the right place to be.

There was no one left in Caitlin's life that she had that kind of connection to. Of course she had friends. But nothing like the relationship she could see in front of her now, and it left her feeling a little empty inside.

Caitlin pulled up some other screens on her tablet and took Natalia through the operation, step by step. There were more questions, and she got the sense that Natalia needed some time to process.

She put her hand on Natalia's arm. 'This is a lot to take in, and I want you to take some time to think about everything. Like I told you earlier, I am always around if you have questions. Just tell one of the nursing staff to page me.'

Natalia gave a nod of her head. 'Thank you for this.'

Caitlin gave another nod, keeping her hand gently on Natalia's arm. 'The final decision on this rests with you. I can only give you my recommendation for surgery. I need to know that you understand all of this fully, before we continue.'

Natalia took a deep breath. 'I know you're the best at this. If this is what you think, then this is what we'll do. I'll let you know if I have questions.'

Caitlin stood up. Part of her felt relieved that Natalia clearly understood the procedures and the associated risks. But she recognised it was time to step away and give her time to think.

She gave Natalia a nod at the doorway, 'Let's talk later.'

She started to walk down the corridor but had made it only a few steps before she felt a hand on her arm. 'Cait—'

She spun around. Javier. The shadows under his eyes looked even darker out here.

'Can we talk?' The strain was evident in his voice and she felt a pang of sadness. She didn't like seeing him like this.

'Will you have a coffee with me?'

She'd said no before. But that had been about them. This was about his sister, his family member, who was about to undergo major surgery that came with associated risks. If this had been any other patient she wouldn't hesitate to sit down with their concerned relatives. How could she say no to him?

She gave the briefest nod. 'Let's find a quiet corner in the canteen,' she agreed.

Javier's thoughts were racing. He had a million questions. Not that he was disagreeing with the principles behind Caitlin's decision-making and her request for further testing. He knew they would be sound. But he needed to understand them himself. He wanted to know that, faced with the same set of facts, he would make the same decision about his sister.

Part of him wished she'd told him first. But they'd lost the familiarity they'd once had, and Caitlin would always put her patient first. He knew that too.

That was the thing about knowing someone as well as you knew yourself. He couldn't help but regret the fact that they'd lost that.

Before he even had a chance to think, Caitlin had bought two coffees and was gesturing with her head for him to follow her.

She walked to the back of the canteen, near a wall of windows that looked out over St Aelina's park.

Javier sat down opposite her and shook his head. 'This is getting to be a habit.'

'What is?'

'You footing the bill. It has to stop. You know it drives me crazy.'

'Maybe that's why I'm doing it.'

And with those words he felt his body sag. This was the way they used to talk together. 'Banter' Caitlin had always called it. And it was the first bit of normality he'd felt in so long. For the first time since he'd got here he finally felt relaxed.

'I know you're concerned.' Her voice was calm and steady. She turned her tablet back to face him. 'Here are the test results. Natalia said I can share them. Take your time.'

So he did. He read everything that she had. It didn't take him long to see exactly why she'd come to the decision she had.

He pushed the tablet back to her. 'Okay.'

Caitlin looked him in the eyes. Those green eyes were brighter than he could ever remember. Fascinating. Mesmerising.

He pulled his gaze away and looked out across the park. A few parents were there with strollers, pushing their children on the swings. In another corner with benches he could see some older residents putting the world to rights.

'I'm glad you did those other tests—and suggest the new ones. Without them we wouldn't have known what we do now, and I appreciate you taking time to confirm everything.'

They were relatively new tests and not every clinician used them. But one had shown the strain on the cardiac muscles. It had shown how even a tiny bit of regurgitation from one of Natalia's valves was having detrimental effects, and how quickly these would exacerbate.

'That's why you recommended me to look after your sister, Javier. That's why you know she's in good hands.'

He leaned forward and put his head in his hands for a second, running his fingers through his short hair. When he lifted his head he met her gaze. 'I just want to say that I understand the risks. I know that something can happen. And if it does I know it won't be down to you.'

Caitlin flinched and blinked. Her eyes looked watery, as if she were trying to keep tears back. She shook her head determinedly. 'It won't happen. Don't think like that.'

He wanted to reach across and touch her hand. But something stopped him. Every time their skin had come into contact since he'd got here it had been like a lightning bolt to his heart. It just took him back to that night together. The one imprinted on his brain.

The one he definitely wanted to repeat.

For a second their gazes clashed again, and tiny pink spots appeared on Caitlin's cheeks. She turned her head quickly to the park. Had she been reliving their night together, just like he had?

He swallowed. If he could turn back the clock he would. He'd been confused that morning when they'd woken wrapped in each other's arms. Caitlin had seemed to brush the whole thing off, and he'd known deep down that his life would eventually take him in a completely different direction. And that direction was about to hit home even more imminently now. He would have to step up. He would have to step away from his patients in Madrid. Things would be confusing. He'd never learned the business on the estate the way that his sister had, so the learning curve would be steep. But he had to be there. He had to make sure she made a good recovery from her surgery; he had to protect her in a way she'd never needed before. So, sitting here and thinking about a naked Caitlin, the feel of her skin next to his, the smell of fruit shampoo from her hair, or of the moisturiser she used on her skin that reminded him of sunshine, the touch of her soft lips on his, was all too much of a distraction right now.

He pushed those thoughts from his brain. That wouldn't help him now. He had to stop thinking about Caitlin the ex-lover, and think only of Caitlin the expert cardiothoracic surgeon.

There. He could do that. If he had the right mind frame just being in her company helped. She grounded him.

He'd watched her with his sister and admired how good she was with her patients, compassionate, factual and accessible. Everything that could be desired in a clinician.

It was as if she read his mind—or needed a distraction, just like him. She flicked something else up on her tablet. 'So, we're both night shift. One of the first things you mentioned to me was that you were here to help me get the waiting list down. How would you feel about fitting some surgeries in?'

He leaned forward, interested.

'I have a small waiting list. These are more

complicated surgeries that I knew would need assistance from another experienced surgeon. My trainees are great, but they're not quite there. So, apart from any emergencies, how would you feel if we scheduled a few of these surgeries while you are here?'

He smiled, glad that she'd brought it up. 'How will your patients feel about an unconventional surgery time?'

'They will just be glad to have it scheduled. You, myself and my staff are all scheduled for night shifts. We won't be over-tired. We will be prepared. I'm sure we can make this work.'

Javier gave a nod. This was perfect. It would keep his mind on the job, instead of fretting over his sister constantly. The surgeries sounded challenging. He was happy to assist. In fact, he wanted to.

'Introduce me to your first patient then,' he said with renewed vigour.

Her smile broadened as she pulled up a patient history. 'Okay,' she started. 'Jean Bishop, fifty-six-year-old male with a history of previously undiagnosed Kawasaki disease…'

They bent their heads together and started discussing the case.

CHAPTER FOUR

It was late in the evening. Javier was pounding the running track around the very impressive park next to St Aelina's. He hadn't really wanted to admit how good the park was to Caitlin, but it was certainly a big draw for the staff. The whole vibe of St Aelina's was around staff health and wellbeing. He noticed that whilst on duty staff spoke about the gym and the swimming pool. Most attended some of the affiliated classes—yoga, spin. There was even a book group that apparently was very well attended, with usually lots of discussion around their book choices.

He liked that about this place; he admired it. Whilst he loved his own hospital in Madrid, it did have a more traditional outlook. Several of the hospital staff were the sons or daughters of consultants or surgeons who had worked there before. Although no one had ever suggested it, he wondered if his status as a Count had helped with the job offer he'd received. He knew Caitlin hadn't applied to the Madrid training programme, but would a poor girl from Scotland have been offered a place—even if she was the most brilliant trainee? He didn't even want to contemplate what the answer might be, because he knew he wouldn't like it.

Being here was giving him a new outlook, a fresh perspective. Had his life been so insular in Madrid that he hadn't stopped to consider other things?

He heard running footsteps approaching rapidly from behind. Two seconds later Caitlin jogged past. 'Do you always run this slow?' she threw over her shoulder.

He laughed and quickened his pace to catch her. She was wearing a set of dark grey running gear, her auburn hair in a ponytail on top of her head that bobbed as she ran.

'Not everything has to be a race,' he said as he easily caught up with her. 'Some of us are in it for the long haul.'

After a few moments she turned her head to look at him as she kept running. 'But you're not any more, are you?'

Her words came out of the blue and his footsteps stumbled, slowing him down to a stop.

She stopped next to him, leaning over and breathing heavily.

He looked at her, his chest tight because he'd stopped so suddenly. 'What makes you say that?'

She stood up and put her hands on her hips. 'I've been thinking about it some more. 'I can't believe you're even contemplating leaving.'

Neither could he. And it was the last thing in the world he wanted to do. But it felt disloyal saying it.

'Family comes first.'

She blinked and pressed her lips together. He knew her family circumstances had never been great, so maybe it wasn't a fair thing to say. But it was the truth, and he had to lay it on the line. He would do anything to try and ensure his sister's health.

Caitlin sighed and looked off sideways towards the lit-up city. He couldn't take his eyes from the pale line of skin from her throat and neck, leading down to the scoop of her top. He'd good memories of that part of her skin.

'I get that,' she said, her voice a little throaty. 'But I don't like it.'

She was being blunt. Caitlin had spent most of her life teasing him, but this was different. She was blunt when she was annoyed, or verging on angry.

He bent over and put his hands on his knees. There was so much pressure on him right now. He hadn't had the time to talk things through with anyone. Because he had no choice in all of this. Javier Torres would always do the right thing.

His colleagues in Madrid had been dismayed when he'd had the initial conversation, as a starting point, to break the news that he might have to leave.

He'd started to be copied in to numerous emails about the family business and estate. It was overwhelming. He actually didn't know where to start, because he hadn't paid that much attention before. There was so much he didn't know—even though it had always been part of his life.

He knew the people, the generations of families that worked at Maravilla. At least that worked in his favour. Except it didn't. Because those families relied on the continued success of the business for their livelihood. What if Javier got there and made stupid decisions because he just didn't know better?

What if he got something wrong about the grape harvest and wiped out a year's worth of work?

There was so much at stake. Not just the picking of the grapes and fruits at exactly the right time, but all the processes that followed that too. Every one of them had a crucial failure point. How could he even begin to explain all this to Caitlin? She had such a different background from him. Would she even begin to understand?

'We don't always have the choices we would want,' he replied, and she turned around, glaring at him with hostile eyes.

'I think you haven't looked at other opportunities. There must be something else you could do. Bring in a new manager. An assistant. You don't have to do it yourself.'

He reached over and put his hands on her arms. 'No one else is the Conde de Maravilla. That's me, Caitlin. It's my job. My inheritance. My responsibility.'

He sighed and looked up at the dark sky. 'I've been living on borrowed time. I knew eventually my father would expect me to return and take over. I probably should have done it a few years ago, when he died. But Natalia was very determined. She's worked on the estate all her life. It's much more hers than mine. And when she told me everything was under control, and I could continue what I was doing, I was delighted.'

He was still touching her arms and she was staring at him with those big green eyes. 'I shirked my responsibility then; I won't shirk it now.'

Caitlin tilted her head. 'There's no talking you out of this, is there?' She lifted one of her hands and touched a finger to his cheek. It was a delicate movement.

'No,' he said, so quietly it was almost a whisper.

'So you'll be here the next few weeks, and then that's it?'

He nodded and their gazes locked. He could feel his heart sizzle in his chest. He wanted to stay right here, in this moment in time with Caitlin. When they were both surgeons in the same city together, and they might finally have a chance to reconnect.

Some people got a second chance in life. Might they?

Caitlin was still annoyed. She'd finished her run with Javier yesterday evening and they'd said goodnight, agreeing to meet this morning for breakfast at his hotel.

She wasn't quite sure why she'd agreed to meet here. She'd never eaten in a hotel like this before and as she walked through the lobby she felt strangely out of step.

The concierge greeted her and showed her to the elevator, taking her to the top floor, where the bar was situated. Javier was sitting at a table waiting for her. He smiled and stood up. 'I thought we might have breakfast in the sunshine and enjoy the views.' She nodded and sat down next to him.

She'd heard about this rooftop bar, and seen the occasional celebrity snap from up here, but it was the first time she'd been here herself. Its outlook across the city was incredible. Fourteen floors above the city gave a view of most of the surrounding area—even better than the view from the helipad on top of St Aelina's. The view of the Sagrada Familia was impressive, even though it was far away. Looking the other way, she could see the cruise ships coming into Barcelona with their thousands of eager tourists and the sparkling blue ocean.

She settled back in her chair, giving the waiter her order and accepting some coffee and orange juice while they were waiting. She opened the folder she'd brought with her, with the list of patients.

'So, we have three already scheduled. But let's look at the others. I can get them in for their pre-op assessments in the next few days, so we can get up-to-date bloods and scans.'

'You haven't already done those? At my hospital we do those before we even discuss the patients.'

She was irked by the implied criticism. The words 'at my hospital' certainly didn't help.

She gave her best smile. 'At my hospital I don't start pre-operative assessments on patients I haven't completely decided to schedule for surgery. It creates a false expectation if you do that, don't you think? Imagine knowing you have a condition; you come in, get a complete pre-op assessment, bloods, scan, thinking that they're going to give you a date for surgery, and instead you get an "I'm sorry, you're not really suitable for surgery".' She raised her eyebrows. 'Imagine how devastating that is for your patients.'

'It would be,' said Javier smoothly, 'if it had ever happened. But at *my* hospital I know from first referral if someone will be suitable or not. If they're not, they simply don't proceed any further.'

Caitlin leaned back and folded her arms. 'That sounds like a very unthorough approach. Doesn't every patient deserve a full assessment?'

Javier could clearly sense she was baiting him. 'Only if they are suitable for surgery.'

'And you can tell by your X-ray vision and your clear ability to know someone's blood results just by looking at them?'

The waiter appeared and set down their breakfast plates, quickly retreating as he looked at the expressions on their faces.

Caitlin looked down at her perfectly cooked poached eggs on toast. She wanted to dive in. But she wanted to win this argument first. If he said the words *my hospital* again in that smooth, smug accent he might find himself wearing them.

He gave a soft laugh. 'Granted, I don't quite have space age technology yet. But let's be reasonable; do you really think it is that far off? I bet in the next few years we'll be able to get a full set of blood readings from a finger prick.'

'Maybe,' she agreed. 'But you still can't

tell just by looking at a patient. No one is that good.'

The words were like a challenge across the table, and Javier gave her a smile. 'I guess we'll wait and see.'

'What about all the questions you've been asking my staff?'

He looked surprised. 'What do you mean?'

A few of her staff members had mentioned how friendly Javier had been, asking lots of questions about processes in the cardiothoracic unit and the rationale around some of the protocols that had been developed. It had started to make her wonder if he was actually checking up on her—checking up on them all—before Natalia's surgery.

'They told me you've been asking questions about lots of things.'

'Wouldn't you expect me to? I need to be up to speed about what's normal in your unit. I'd hate to find out that you routinely order a particular test and I've missed it, or that you use particular wound dressings or drugs. We all have our favourites. I'm just making sure I'm consistent with the approach you take at St Aelina's.'

'So why not just ask me?' It was a simple question. She would have happily talked Javier through everything he needed to know. She'd already left checklists of particular procedures that included all this information in the patient records she'd left for him to study.

'You're too busy. You have so much else going on. I'm trying to be a help, not a hindrance.'

'Feels like you're checking up on me.' The words came out automatically.

This time it was Javier who leaned back in his chair, his face serious. 'I don't need to check up on you. I brought my sister here because I thought you, and your staff, were the best. Should I doubt that?'

'Do you doubt that?' she countered. 'Is that the reason for all the questions?'

He gave a soft laugh and his dark brown eyes met hers. He was exasperated with her, obviously realising this was a fight that, no matter how he answered, he couldn't win. 'I'm satisfied with everything I've seen,' he said firmly.

She nodded. Nagging doubts still filled her. Along with a whole host of thoughts as to how she might be acting if this was a relative of hers, and their roles were reversed. Truth was, Caitlin might actually be a thou-

sand times worse than Javier was being. The
nurses had been flattered by his attention,
and it irked her that it could be another reason
why his questions had annoyed her.

Javier lifted her lists and looked over them
critically, getting straight to the point. 'This
patient, Luis Carrero, wouldn't you just do a
direct replacement valve?'

Caitlin picked up her knife and fork, determined to have at least one bite of her poached
eggs before she launched them across the
table towards him.

'Look at his cardiac scan in detail. There's
minor heart muscle damage. There's something else going on with this man.'

Javier leaned over to take in more information as Caitlin took a sip of the surprisingly
good coffee. 'Wow,' she said in appreciation.

'I had them mix it for you,' he said without looking up.

'You did what?'

'That coffee you used to like—I remembered the blend and asked for it this morning.'

She was quietly stunned. 'You remembered
coffee from all those years ago?'

He gave a nonchalant shrug. 'Some things
stick with you.'

Caitlin pressed her lips together. There had been an old French coffee shop down the road from the university that she'd loved. The coffee from that shop had been her wakeup call in the morning. 'I always thought that place had superpowers.' She smiled, remembering. 'As soon as I tasted that stuff it was like my brain switched on and everything fell into place.'

Javier gave a nod. 'I asked about the blend, years ago, and always remembered.' He lifted his cup. 'Is it close enough for you?'

'It's perfect,' she agreed, still shocked at his thoughtfulness. That was the thing about Javier. He'd always managed to surprise her. They could be fighting one minute during their studies, arguing over the best way to complete a procedure or the diagnosis of a potential case, then the next moment he would appear with food for them both, or chocolates, or sometimes just a crate of beer.

It seemed that even though a number of years had passed, they were still as connected as before. It was unnerving. And she wasn't quite sure she was ready for it.

She leaned back further in her chair, letting the early morning sun heat her skin, and closed the file on the table. These surgeries would be scheduled. She would do things her way, by assessing all patients completely and making the call on appropriate surgery when she was ready to. 'Let's leave this for now,' she said simply. 'After all, these are my patients. I'll tell you what I need you to do.'

She was drawing a line in the sand—just like she knew Javier would if their roles were reversed. He didn't object, just gave her a thoughtful look.

'What else has been going on in your life?' she asked, trying to change the subject.

Javier smiled. 'Apart from life, love, estates and surgery?'

She nodded. 'Have you visited any other hospitals?'

It was something she'd done regularly while working on the new tool for surgery and carrying out her heart valve research. Visiting other specialist hospitals was always useful for getting new ideas and seeing where others were in relation to procedures.

He nodded. 'I've been to Berlin and Los Angeles in the last year. What about you?' He didn't even need to tell her the names of the surgeons he'd met with; she already knew who worked in these hospitals.

'I spent some time in Zurich, and in Ottawa.'

'Canada?'

She nodded. 'I think I'm going to go back there. I met a really interesting surgeon who I'd like to try and poach.'

'You did?' He was clearly amused. Research hospitals were always trying to steal the best staff from each other.

She nodded and gave him a curious glance. 'So, what else has happened in your life?'

He gave another shrug. 'My mother tried to get me married off. It didn't work. I guess I'm just an eternal disappointment to her.'

'You were engaged?'

'You didn't hear?'

'I don't keep up-to-date with gossip magazines or popular news. It's not really my thing,' she admitted. 'Who were you engaged to?'

'Elisabeth—she's a German duchess. Charming lady. Perfect in a lot of ways.'

She should be annoyed right now, but something about the way he said the words struck her as odd. There was no deep, abounding affection in them, more like a fondness.

'And it didn't work out?'

He shook his head. 'Much to my parents' disappointment. They loved her.'

Caitlin's heart sank. A German duchess would be a very suitable wife for a Spanish count—unlike a girl from a council flat in Glasgow. Elisabeth and Javier sounded like a match made in heaven.

'And you didn't?'

He flinched, her words clearly striking a nerve. 'I…liked her very much. And I tried hard to make things work. But could I see myself growing old with her?' He shook his head. 'No, not really. And that matters. She tried too, but something held me back. I just didn't love her the way I was supposed to.'

'But your mother liked her?'

He gave a sad smile. 'My mother still holds out hope that one day we will reconcile. But it will never happen. For lots of reasons.'

He left things there. But Caitlin wanted to ask a dozen more questions.

She kept her mouth closed. It was inevitable there would be many things about Javier she didn't know, after twelve years of being out of touch. But what startled her was how out of sorts that made her feel.

She had no right to expect to know things

about him; she'd actively avoided looking him up in any way. But now something was burrowing away at her, making her feel annoyed—as if she had a right to know about Javier's life.

What on earth was wrong with her?

She gave a signal to the waiter to top up her coffee. If Javier had gone to the trouble of finding her favourite from long ago, then the least she could do was drink it.

She gave him a smile. 'We don't always do what our parents expect of us. Doesn't make us bad people.'

He raised one eyebrow. 'Your parents have been in touch?'

She shrugged her shoulders. 'My mother wants me to buy her a flat somewhere. My father wants me to give him money to pay off gambling debts. I'm basically just a chequebook to them.'

She could see him hesitate before he spoke. 'And…have you done it?'

She shook her head, knowing she was unable to hide the sad expression on her face. 'Nothing has changed. They're still not interested in me. And I'm big enough not to allow myself to be used.'

Something crossed Javier's face, and the

edges of his lips moved upwards in an approving, sympathetic smile. He raised his coffee cup towards her. 'And that's why we are friends.'

A warm feeling swept over her and she lifted her newly filled cup in response. 'Friends,' she agreed.

CHAPTER FIVE

THEIR WORKING ASSOCIATION continued so easily. The long discussions over complicated patients. The pre-operative assessments, and the scheduling at short notice of these patients.

The relief from the patients and their relatives was palpable. They were getting two expert surgeons to perform their operations.

Caitlin was surprised at how comfortable she felt around Javier again. She couldn't pretend that the attraction wasn't still there; she could still feel the underlying buzz. But she could also ignore it and let her brain focus entirely on her patients and their care.

There was still that tiny underlying feeling that he might be checking up on her. That he was watching her practice in order to make sure she was as good as he hoped she was.

But in some ways she could understand this. Natalia was his sister. He was worried.

And she wasn't entirely sure she would be any different if she'd had a brother or sister in a similar position.

She'd ordered another few tests for Natalia, and was happy to let Javier feel involved in the treatment plan. After all, once surgery was over, he would be the person who would be closest to his sister to monitor her ongoing condition.

She wondered how he would manage that— whether he would want Natalia transferred back to Madrid or transferred back to the family home. They hadn't discussed that yet, but they would. She wanted to oversee all of Natalia's care, including her recovery. She was sure that, at some point, Javier would want to discuss all that with her. Right now, his focus was on the surgery, and she got that. But soon they would need to go over the possibility that Natalia might require some time for rehabilitation.

She was already getting feedback on Javier. People liked him. There had been the inevitable comments about him being easy on the eye. But people were also talking about his amiable manner and his extensive knowledge. He'd been asked for a few consults, and colleagues had been complimentary about him taking his time, being thorough, looking at all contributing factors and giving recommendations.

She'd even had a few curious queries about whether he was attached or not. Those had made her bristle, which had surprised her. Twelve years was a long time. But she couldn't deny the way she felt when she was in the same room as him. It was as if every cell in her body remembered him. Remembered the electricity between them, and what his touch could do to her. It had been a long time since she'd been distracted at work with thoughts like those.

The night-time surgeries had so far proved a success. Two patients had been operated on, and both were still in hospital and recovering well. Her pager sounded, just as they were about to review files for the next patient.

Javier looked up from his screen. 'Want some help?'

She glanced at her pager. 'It's the ER. Another chest injury from an RTA.'

They headed for the stairwell and went down to the department. It wasn't quite as busy as the last time they'd been there, but Marco was on duty again.

'You might want to meet this one in the bay again,' he said. 'Isabella has radioed in that she thinks it's a flail chest with cardiac complications.'

They looked at each other. Normally a trauma surgeon would deal with a flail chest, but if there were cardiac complications both were happy to assist.

They ran out to the bay just as the ambulance pulled in and Isabella Rivas threw open the back doors. She jumped down, efficient as always. Caitlin started walking alongside the stretcher. 'Isabella Rivas, this is Javier Torres, a visiting surgeon.'

'Pleasure,' said Isabella quickly. 'Francesca Corien, thirty-seven. HGV collided with her car. I suspect a flail chest and cardiac complications.' She nodded at the monitor, where the heart rate was erratic.

'No problem,' said Caitlin automatically, 'we've got this.'

She trusted Isabella, a more than capable paramedic who was extremely efficient. She missed nothing, and often picked up on things that others might not have noticed. If Isabella suspected a cardiac complication, she would be right.

Their patient was visibly ill; a flail chest

was a devastating injury, caused by direct impact on the chest wall and resulting in ribs fracturing and leading to other injuries.

'Pneumothorax,' said Javier as he listened to Francesca's chest and turned around to open a pack and insert a chest tube.

'Same this side,' said Caitlin as she also set up a pack. The radiographer wheeled in the machine for the portable X-ray and they pulled lead aprons over their heads for a few moments. Once it was completed, the X-ray was automatically sent to the screen at their side. There were no surprises; it was exactly what they'd expected. Isabella was still there; she always waited that extra few seconds to make sure her patients were settled and in good hands. The ER could be chaotic at times, and it wouldn't be the first time Caitlin had walked into the resus room to see Isabella calmly assisting.

She gave her a smile. 'Did you enjoy your last few days of good surf weather?'

Everyone knew that Isabella was a skilful surfer. She'd taught a few colleagues to ride the waves and normally talked about her hobby with complete passion. But today she was strangely quiet. She gave a small nod. 'Everything's good here. I'll leave it all with you.'

She lowered her head and walked out, making Caitlin curious as to what was wrong. But she didn't have time to think about it much as she continued to open packs.

The technician next to them did her best to try and get a heart tracing while they prepared. Marco administered some pain relief to their patient and made sure her airway was clear and oxygen in place. 'You go first,' said Caitlin, standing back for a few minutes to let Javier insert the tube to reinflate Francesca's left lung.

Javier did the procedure expertly. There was no hesitation, no hanging around. After some local anaesthetic was injected, it was a simple neat incision and the tube was in place and connected. Caitlin did hers next. It only took another few minutes. Once they had both listened to the lungs and were satisfied they were inflated, Caitlin took a transducer and pressed it lightly on Francesca's chest wall. She had to get a view of the heart. The monitor continued to show runs of dangerous extra beats.

'Tamponade?' asked Javier, already taking a needle from a nearby trolley.

Caitlin nodded as she watched the image on the screen. It was definite cardiac tamponade. The pericardium that surrounded the heart was filled with extra fluid—likely blood—that was stopping it beating properly. This was a life-threatening injury.

She moved around to the other side and bent her head next to Javier's, their faces brushing against each other as Javier carefully guided the needle into the pericardial sac to withdraw some of the fluid. She wasn't thinking about anything other than their patient.

But she couldn't ignore the feel of his stubble next to her cheek. As he steadily withdrew the fluid from the heart she couldn't help but turn her face slightly towards his. Last time they'd been this close they'd been kissing.

'Well done,' she whispered, aware that he might be thinking the same thing.

There was a twinkle deep within his dark eyes. So much emotion. So much depth. She turned her gaze back to the dark red fluid being withdrawn, saving Francesca's life.

Caitlin let out a deep breath as she straightened up, her eyes on the monitor. Almost immediately Francesca's heart rate started to steady. 'We need to make sure that doesn't happen again. Is there a bed available in Coronary Care?'

One of the ER nurses nodded. 'I've asked the ward sister to come down. I want to give her a complete handover and I'd like her to take the patient back up to the unit.'

Marie, the night sister, came down a few minutes later. She was completely unfazed by the two chest tubes, and the other lines and equipment which had been put in place to support Francesca. She took the handover easily and nodded to Caitlin and Javier. 'Another dream team job finished. You two better watch out. Everyone is saying how well you work together.'

They exchanged a glance, and there it was again. That shiver across her skin. As Marie headed down the corridor with their patient and one of the porters, Javier gave her a look that could have no other meaning.

'Let's tidy up,' he said through almost clenched teeth.

'Sure,' she said, clearing the clinical trolley and disposing of everything while her eyes never really left his.

It was like doing some strange kind of dance. They watched each other every step of the way, as they tidied the resus room, quickly resupplying what had been used, then disposing of their gloves, aprons and masks and washing their hands.

The clean-up must have taken a whole two minutes but it seemed like so much longer.

Side by side, they started to walk down the corridor, but finally it proved too much for Javier and he grabbed her by the elbow and pulled her into one of the large storage cupboards.

She laughed as he pressed her against the metal shelf rack, his arm at the side of her head. She didn't even get a chance to speak before he kissed her.

And there it was.

The sensation she'd relived a million times. The memories came flooding back. Instinctively, Caitlin wrapped her arms around his neck and kissed him passionately. It had been too long. One of his hands slid up her side, the palm slipping under the scrub top and coming into contact with her skin.

Caitlin sucked in a breath and Javier stopped, pulling his lips back from hers. It had been seconds, and she couldn't believe the wave of regret at that single movement.

'Okay?' he queried. 'Am I going too fast?'

'I want to say no,' she said, smiling and

grabbing the edges of his scrub top and kissing him again. This time she made herself pull back. 'But I don't think we should do this in here.'

It was an odd sensation because they'd never officially been lovers, they'd never had stolen moments like this before. They'd laughed and joked about colleagues being caught in compromising positions. No matter how many sensations were overwhelming her right now, her reputation here was untarnished. Shouldn't she try to keep it that way?

She took his hand. 'Walk this way.'

She strode down the corridor with Javier at her side. If anyone noticed the hand-holding nothing was said. They didn't even attempt to wait for an elevator, just ran up the four flights of stairs and strode quickly to Caitlin's office. She turned the lock on the door as soon as they were inside.

This time it was her who pushed Javier back against the door. 'Where were we?'

He smiled and pulled his top over his head. 'Somewhere about here.'

Her body reacted to his every touch, her clothes disappearing like his, all while their lips remained connected, making her laugh at their movements. All she knew right now was that she didn't want their lips to part again.

They fumbled back towards her large sofa as his kisses moved down her neck. 'Not sure you're doing my heart rate any good,' she laughed.

'It's an assessment,' he murmured, his mouth barely leaving her skin.

'How am I doing?' she whispered as his mouth moved lower.

'Top marks,' came the response.

Two hours later they were in a familiar position, limbs entwined, with no clothing left. 'So, now we're talking again,' asked Javier in a lazy voice, 'can we talk?'

Caitlin looked at him, a small furrow across her brow. 'What do you want to talk about?'

He ran a finger along her side. She flinched and let out a giggle. 'Stop that.'

'I'm making up for lost time.' The words struck a chord with her and she gave a sad kind of smile, a far-off look on her face.

Javier ran his fingers through her hair, coming back to stroke her cheek. 'Why did we take so long to get together? Six years of being rivals, one explosive night and then...'

Caitlin lifted her hand to cover his. 'Let's not talk about the past. There's no point.'

He shook his head. 'But there is. I want more than this, Caitlin, and so do you.'

She closed her eyes for a moment, willing a million things away. The fact that he was a Count, the fact that she came from a place that could never be part of his world. In here, tonight, they were equals. But that was the only place.

'We're too different, Javier. I'm never going to measure up as a Countess—and I'm not sure I want to. I can't forget about where I was brought up, or how hard I had to work to get away from there. It's made me who I am.'

'And I think you're perfect.'

'Perfect for now. Perfect for this moment. But not for the future. I'd never want to leave this job for a life on a country estate—no matter how spectacular it is.'

'And I would never ask you to,' he countered quickly.

There was a tiny twist deep inside. Did he also think she wouldn't measure up?

'Why won't you let your guard down with me, Caitlin? You know me. You know who I am. Why won't you just trust me with your feelings?'

She gave a sigh and opened her eyes again. This close, those deep brown eyes made her feel as if she could lose her very soul to him. 'Trust is hard,' she admitted. 'You know my mum and dad flitted in and out of my life. But my dad was controlling. He was a liar and a cheat. My mother had a miserable marriage, and eventually she broke free and started to act exactly the way that he had. It was like her own secret revenge. And I was the pawn in the middle. I can never let that happen. I've always sworn that would never happen to me—I'd never let a man control me like that.'

'And you think I would be like that?' His voice was incredulous.

She took a deep breath. And maybe it would have been better to be upright and fully clothed, but it was too late now. 'I know what your parents' wishes were, Javier. I know you feel as if you have a duty and responsibility to fill—especially now that Natalia is unwell, and I can't guarantee her outcome.' It was her turn to stroke his face. 'I'll never be the Countess.' She smiled as she said it, because she knew just how true those words were. 'And that's fine. Because I have most of the life that I want here. My career, my home. I'm not an ancestral estate kind of girl. I don't want to move in high society circles. I have no idea who the important people are in Europe, and I have no wish to learn. As for winemaking? I'm happy to occasionally drink the stuff, but I want to learn more about cardiac muscles, not vineyards.'

He gave a long slow nod of his head. She could tell that he knew everything she said was true, and she was glad he didn't try to make excuses or tell her she was wrong.

'So, what do we do?' he whispered.

Caitlin took a breath. This felt easier than she'd expected it to. She'd forgotten how grounded he made her. How safe he made her feel.

She ran her fingers over his short hair. For a few moments Javier Torres actually felt like hers. 'I vote that we make the most of the here and now. What have we got—another few weeks? Why don't we use them wisely?'

The tone of his voice changed, along with the glint in his eyes. He ran one tantalising finger down the length of her spine. 'I think you should show me how you want to proceed.'

She tipped back her head and revealed the pale skin of her neck to him again. 'I absolutely agree.'

CHAPTER SIX

THEY'D MADE A PLAN. It was just under a week until Natalia's surgery and both had a few days off.

Caitlin tipped her head back and rubbed her eyes as they walked out into the sunlight. 'I think I'm a vampire,' she groaned. 'The thing I hate most about nights is the transition back to days.'

'Well, you're the best-looking vampire I've ever seen,' joked Javier as he sat her wide-brimmed hat on her auburn hair. 'Are you ready to hit the beach?'

'Absolutely.' They walked along the Ramblas, stopping at some of the stalls as Caitlin warned him to keep a hold of his wallet, and eventually headed down to the strip of beach. He knew, as a pale-skinned Scot, sun wasn't really Caitlin's thing, but she'd insisted on taking a walk down to the beach instead of going to the more crowded tourist attractions across Barcelona.

And he hadn't been joking; she looked incredible. She was wearing denim shorts, a short-sleeved yellow shirt, knotted at her waist, her wide-brimmed hat and a pair of flat sandals. Caitlin was a runner—she'd already shown Javier the route she favoured throughout the nearby park and streets of Barcelona. She'd always been a runner and, with her height, her athletic body couldn't help but attract a few glances.

As they walked, she slathered her arms in sunblock, chatting sometimes in English and sometimes in Spanish. Her Spanish had improved greatly since living in Barcelona. She'd learned basic Spanish whilst being regularly in Javier's company, and from visiting his family home. But now she'd learned the things you could only learn when you lived in a place, the local dialect, the lilt to certain words. She was a natural.

He reached over and took her hand, but Caitlin moved closer and slipped an arm around his waist. 'I prefer this—' she gave him a quiet smile '—then I get to put my head on your shoulder when I'm tired.'

He put his arm around her too and let the

warm feeling spread over him. It was as if the connection had never really left them, and he wanted to drink it in for as long as he could.

His mother had already phoned this morning, with a few estate issues. She'd been asking him to make decisions he didn't feel qualified or experienced enough to make, but he understood exactly why she didn't want to ask Natalia at this time.

'Can it wait?' he'd asked in exasperation, part of him wondering if his mother was trying to give him a taste of what was to come.

'I suppose so,' she'd pondered.

'Then it should wait,' he'd said firmly. 'You have to let me do what I do best right now, and that's be a surgeon. I need to focus on Natalia now, and I get to stay here by being a surgeon.'

His mother had relented and he was grateful. He didn't want to think about vine orders or harvesting times and processes right now. He wanted to concentrate on Caitlin. The time here was precious. He'd waited twelve years for this and didn't want to waste a second.

They bought takeaway coffee and fruit and lay on the beach under a parasol for a few hours. Then they drifted back towards the heart of Barcelona and found a bar that served sangria and bar snacks.

Caitlin stretched her legs out as they waited for their food. 'I don't get to do this often enough,' she sighed.

'Too busy with work?'

She nodded and smiled. 'I know you get it. We become immersed in things, and even though I mean to take time to go to the cinema, or read books or go for more dinners, it always comes back to those little things that prey on your mind. You know what I mean?'

He laughed. 'Oh, the *I'll just check those test results*, or *I'll just read that research study*, or *I'll just email a colleague at another hospital about work they've done on something*?'

She pointed her finger at him in jest. 'You get it!'

The waiter set down their jug of sangria and poured it into glasses for them.

'Okay,' said Javier in a low voice, because he loved how she looked right now—totally relaxed, her auburn hair tumbling over her shoulders and a tiny bit of colour in her cheeks. 'If I could wave a magic wand and this whole day was your own—let's imagine you didn't have to entertain a visiting surgeon and could spend it on anything but work. What would you do?'

Caitlin closed her eyes as she took a sip of the sangria. 'Hmm, let's think. Anything at all...' She kept her eyes closed.

Javier tried his best not to concentrate on those long legs, but it was harder work than he was willing to commit to. 'Anything at all,' he murmured in return.

'In that case, I'll use your magic wand and fly to Trinity College in Dublin and spend the afternoon walking around the dreamy Library, then I'll fly to New York and go up the Empire State Building, then fly to London and go to that posh hotel for afternoon tea.' She opened her eyes and gave him a wink. 'Your magic wand will be working overtime.'

She was playing with him, and he liked it. 'Wow, busy day. Don't you ever... I don't know...just relax?' He couldn't help the teasing tone in his voice.

She leaned forward across the small table towards him. 'Relax? From the master of relaxation?' Now she was teasing him even more. 'Tell me, Javier, what do you do to relax? An eight-hour surgery? A ten-K run?'

He held up his hands. 'Okay, you got me. Guilty as charged.' He liked this. He liked the teasing, the familiarity. And, even though they were joking about relaxing, it was clear to him this was the most relaxed either of them had been in a long time.

She reached her fingers towards his, clasping his hand. 'Actually, this has been kind of nice.'

'It has?' His hand folded over hers. She was right. This was nice. It was making him think of things he might have missed out on. It was making him understand why his heart had never been able to commit fully to Elisabeth. It was making him wish these few days or weeks could stretch into months or maybe even years.

'Maybe I would settle for this,' she said simply. *Settle*. Something about the word unnerved him a little. Was she really enjoying herself? Or was he reading this situation wrongly?

But she was smiling at him through her long eyelashes, leaning just far enough forward that he could see a hint of her cleavage.

He was done for.

It was a lazy lunch and afternoon. Caitlin started to flag with the heat. She was used to spending most of her day in the air-conditioned hospital.

Javier watched her through his dark glasses. This was exactly where he wanted to be, and she was the person he wanted to be with. He picked up his phone and dialled the hotel, leaving a few instructions with the concierge. As they strolled back later through the busy streets he bent down and whispered in her ear. 'I have a surprise for you.'

She smiled but gave him a suspicious glance. 'What is it?'

'Come back to the hotel with me, and you'll find out.'

She started laughing as they kept strolling. 'I've already had that surprise.'

He stopped and turned to face her. 'Caitlin McKenzie, have we ever been on a proper date?'

For a few moments she looked lost for words, then finally, 'Well, no...' she wrinkled her nose '...not really.'

'What's the "not really"?' he asked curiously.

'Our graduation ball; we did go to that together.'

'Yes,' he agreed, 'but it wasn't a proper date.'

She shook her head in agreement. 'No, it wasn't.'

'So—' he waited a few moments as he

studied her face '—how about we make this evening our first proper date?'

There was a curious glint in her eye. 'Now that sounds interesting, but…'

'But what?'

She stepped forward and put both hands on his chest. 'I'm all for a date; I'd like that. But I want to spend as much time with you as possible. We both know that, even though we aren't on call, we could get called into the hospital at any moment.'

He could read her mind. 'So, I might get the impression that you want to cut to the chase.'

Her cheeks were showing definite signs of pink, but she laughed. 'That could be true.'

He moved position and took her hand again. 'Let me promise you that there will be no time-wasting. Although our date will be at the hotel, we won't leave it. We won't waste time going around Barcelona.' He whispered in her ear. 'Let me assure you that this will be a *very* private date.'

'I'm intrigued,' she admitted and squeezed his hand. 'And I'm all for private. Lead the way.'

Caitlin looked around the room. Except it wasn't a room; it was a suite. And she had no wish or desire to know what this kind of suite cost on a daily basis. The rooms were beautifully decorated. The bedroom was huge, there was a second bedroom, along with a sitting room, dressing room, a study and two bathrooms.

'I took the liberty of arranging some things for you—for our date,' he hastened to add.

'What do you mean?'

He gestured towards the open door of one of the bedrooms. Caitlin took a few steps inside and stopped. On the bed in front of her was an array of elegant dresses, carefully positioned. There were also open boxes of shoes in a variety of styles. She walked over and touched the first dress. It was red; not a colour that someone would think of for a woman with auburn hair, but Caitlin did wear red when she wanted to. There was another style in black, one in deep purple, another in green and the last in silver.

A smell drifted towards her and she walked over to the bathroom. Inside, there was a bath already prepared, rose petals on the surface, and the light scent of oranges and jasmine. She smiled. It seemed as if Javier had thought of everything. She walked back to the dresses, holding each one up against her and looking at the reflection in the mirror. She wasn't quite sure which one she wanted to wear, the truth being each one was just as beautiful as the next.

She slipped off her clothes and stepped into the bath. It was warm and soothing. Javier had clearly remembered that the scent of oranges was one of her favourites. She frequently favoured candles, shampoos and oils with the aroma of oranges. He'd joked that one day he'd need to give over some of the vineyard for orange trees just to keep her happy, and a tiny part of her heart had saved those words in a little pocket of her brain as a memory to treasure.

At the time they'd still essentially been sparring partners—and it had been a casual remark, half joking—but for Caitlin it was something to hold onto. When she hadn't been shown much affection or interest by either of her parents, someone saying something so personal and thoughtful was something she clung onto.

By the time she emerged from the bathroom, her hair wrapped in a towel, she found a tray of appetisers in the room, along with a cold glass of rosé wine—another of her favourites. She nibbled at the appetisers and sipped the wine, thinking of how perfect the day seemed.

She dried and styled her hair, half clipping it up, then applied the little make-up she had in her bag and went to pick a dress. It seemed that Javier had remembered another detail. Underwear was now next to the bed, all in a variety of shades to match each of the dresses.

She picked up one of the bras and looked at the label. He'd even got the right size. Caitlin let out a laugh. Maybe she should be offended. Maybe she should feel controlled. But Javier was never like that.

This was pure and utter thoughtfulness and generosity. She'd always said no in the past. But this was special. It was their first official date, and she would have been unprepared otherwise.

After a few moments' contemplation, Caitlin picked the red dress. She liked the colour and, no matter what others might think, it did complement her hair. The luxurious fabric slipped over her skin, clinging to all the right places. The back lowered in a dangerous dip, and the skirt reached the floor.

Caitlin took a final sip of her rosé wine and walked through to the main room. Javier was waiting, in a black tuxedo, with a single red rose in his hand.

She couldn't stop smiling as she walked towards him. His eyes didn't leave her for a second. 'Stunning,' was the only word he said as she moved effortlessly into his arms, his hand resting at the dip of fabric near the base of her spine.

He sucked in a deep breath. 'You picked the one I liked the best.'

She kissed him gently on the lips. 'I guess we both have exceedingly good taste—' her hands rested on the top of his arms '—thank you. They were all beautiful. And you know I'll make you send the rest back.'

He pulled her closer towards him. 'Oh, I know. But I wanted you to be happy with what you picked. This is our first date. I've tried to think of everything.'

She slid her arms up around his neck. 'Do we really need to leave the room?'

His grin was broad. 'Only for an hour or so. I think you'll like what comes next.'

He led her to the private elevator that took them down to the second floor. A waiter met them as soon as the doors slid open and showed them down a corridor to a large, dressed room, with one table set in the middle of it, candles flickering in place.

While the lights in the room were dim, one wall had glass doors leading out to a balcony that looked out over Barcelona. It was the same view she had from her office window, and it stretched over the city.

Caitlin looked around, surprised. 'We're the only ones here?'

The waiter gave a quick bow. 'Private dining, as requested. Are you ready for dinner to be served?'

'Yes,' they both said, and then laughed out loud.

Javier held out Caitlin's chair for her to sit, then took the seat opposite. The wine glasses were filled and he lifted his towards her. 'We've agreed to run with this for as long as we're able, so let's keep it simple—to us.'

She picked up her glass and clinked it against his. 'To us.'

His gaze was fixed on hers, and she was glad there were no other guests around them. She wanted privacy with Javier. She wanted to focus her attention only on him.

The rest of the room was virtually empty except for a large grand piano in one corner. 'Did we throw the band out?' she joked.

He glanced over his shoulder and shook his head. 'I asked for it specially.'

'You did?' Now she was surprised. She tried to think back to medical school. She couldn't remember Javier ever playing any instruments—they'd had far too much else to worry about. 'Do you play?'

'We can find out later,' he said with a grin.

The waiter appeared with steaming plates of food and set them down. Caitlin looked at her plate and smiled. 'Do you remember all my favourites?'

He raised his eyebrows. 'I remember them all. But I couldn't ask the chef to make them all.' He leaned forward. 'I think if I'd asked him to do a very British beans on toast he might have spontaneously combusted!'

Caitlin threw back her head and laughed. 'I'll have you know it's still a favourite, but this…' she took a first bite of her food '…is just perfect. Thank you.'

They ate and chatted easily. The first course disappeared quickly, and the main course was another favourite. The wine continued to be topped up, and the sun dipped in the sky outside. Background music played quietly, soft soul music.

'Can you leave the bottle with us, please?'

Javier asked the waiter, who nodded and placed it in the silver bucket next to the table.

'Will there be anything else, *señor*?'

Javier shook his head, and the waiter gave another nod and walked the length of the room. As he left, Caitlin heard the click of a lock.

She could swear a million butterflies just flapped their wings across her skin. They were alone. They had absolute privacy now.

Javier's hand slid across the table and gently closed over Caitlin's. His thumb started circling under the palm of her hand. She closed her eyes for a few moments and let out a deep sigh.

'You're so beautiful,' he said in a low, husky voice.

Caitlin didn't want to wait any longer. She moved out of her chair. Javier stood and lifted their glasses from the table. 'Let's watch the sunset,' he said.

One hand rested comfortably on her hip as they walked over to the full-length doors and stepped out onto the balcony.

The warm evening air was comfortable. Caitlin leaned on the balcony and stared out at the sunset again. 'Well, this is a bit different from our first meeting,' she teased. 'At least my hair is a bit more under control.'

His hand raised automatically to stroke her hair. 'Your hair is always perfect.'

'Charmer,' she teased. 'I bet you say that to all the girls.'

A shadow flitted across his face and he shook his head. 'Only you,' he said in a husky voice as he bent down and kissed her shoulder blade.

She told herself to ignore that look, and not ask herself any questions or wonder. They only had a few weeks together at most. Everything else didn't matter.

Part of her was struggling with this. It was all her daydreaming self had ever wanted, but the time limit seemed like a weight on her shoulders. She couldn't fully enjoy their time together for wondering about when it would end.

'Hey,' he said softly, 'what's wrong?' It was clear he could feel the tension in her body. He held out her arm and started kissing along it.

She sighed and looked out over the beautiful city, silhouetted against the oranges and reds of the sunset. She set down her glass and leaned back into him. 'What could be wrong?' she asked. 'A beautiful city, a perfect date and a wonderful man.'

But Javier could read her better than that. He'd been able to pick up on her stresses about exams, her conflict with her parents and her absolute determination to let nothing get in her way.

His arms slid along the silk of her dress, skirting over her curves. 'How about we try something else?'

'What?' She looked at him curiously as she stepped away. Her blood was already racing around her body, threatening to set her on fire. Last thing she wanted was to put on a display for the world on a balcony overlooking Barcelona. The warm air surrounding her seemed to inflame the heat inside even higher.

'Want to dance?' He stepped back inside the room and held out his arms.

'Last time we danced was at graduation,' she said, as the memory flooded her brain. It had been the build-up of their long-standing attraction. The full-length body contact had left them both in no doubt as to how the evening should end.

'Let's redo things,' he said, and she could hear the tinge of regret in his voice.

Before she had a chance to think more, he'd twirled her under his arm and they'd stepped back inside their private dining room. He took a few steps backwards and held out his arms towards her. Caitlin didn't need to think twice, and she let her body fall into position, putting one hand on his shoulder and the other hand into his. He sighed too as he pulled her body next to his until they were touching all the way down.

'Are we supposed to move?' she said softly into his ear. 'Because I don't want to be apart.' The memories were sparking in her brain again.

'How about we just sway?' came the low voice. And then he moved slowly; it was so easy for her hips to be in unison with his, to feel every part of his body next to hers.

This was all new. They'd never made deliberate moves like this before—last time around it had been much more ad hoc and clumsy—and it made her wonder why she'd wasted the last twelve years. He traced one finger down her spine like he had the other night and she groaned. 'You're killing me.'

'I hope not.'

He moved, turning her around so her back was up against him and his hands were on her stomach, his mouth at her neck. 'How about some other music for my lady?'

Her eyes opened. 'Do you play?' She was curious. But why else would he have asked for a piano?

He took one of her hands again and led her over to the grand piano. She sat down on the large seat next to him as he lifted the lid and stretched his fingers.

'I never told you this,' he said before touching the keys. 'But this is what I do to relax now.' He started to play, and the notes were slow and soothing.

She didn't recognise the tune. But it was soulful, like the music that had been playing around them, which had stopped when he'd started playing. Each note seemed to tell part of a story. He gave her a lazy smile and she wound her foot around his leg.

'Are you trying to distract me?' he asked in a husky voice as he kept playing.

'Absolutely,' came the reply. Her hand slid around his waist and her fingers quickly found a chance to wiggle under his shirt and touch his bare skin. She laughed as he gave a shudder. 'Is it working?'

He looked down and then back at her face. 'Definitely.'

They both laughed, and she stood up behind him and pressed her body against his as she massaged his shoulders. 'I had no idea you did this to relax. When did this start?'

'A few years ago,' he admitted. 'Everything kind of went up in the air. Things were happening back on the estate. My mother and father were putting pressure on me. The hospital wasn't happy because I was being followed by media photographers, so they thought I would be distracted from the job. I went home for a few days and sat down at my old piano. I hadn't played since I'd been a teenager, and I found I loved it again. It made me forget about other things. Made me feel relaxed.'

Her hands were still massaging his shoulders as he spoke. 'What was going on in your life?'

'Nothing important,' he said quickly. 'But I just need some kind of outlet. I wanted you to see it. To hear it.'

She stopped massaging his shoulders and moved back around towards him. She pushed him back a little in his seat so she could step between him and the piano, ignoring the plinks of the keys as she hit a few with her behind.

He looked up at her with those brown eyes. She laid one hand on his cheek. 'You wanted to share this with me?' It suddenly struck her how personal this was for him. How much it meant to him. They'd been out of each other's lives for twelve years. How much more had she missed?

But now he was sharing this with her because it was important to him and he wanted her to know. The similarities between them were like a cloud of hail raining down on her. Just over a week. That was how long they'd been in each other's company again.

She knew that on a personal level she'd lacked that real connection with anyone else over those twelve years—had it been the same for Javier? Was there more to the story about Elisabeth? She was the only woman that he'd mentioned.

Was this why he wanted to share with her now? To let her know something personal about him too?

Whilst they had been good companions and friendly rivals, both had kept quiet about aspects of their own lives. They'd been young then. Now there were no excuses. They were grown-ups. Neither could shy away from their own duties and responsibilities.

He leaned into her hand. 'Who else would I share it with?' he asked.

And that was it. Those were the only words she needed to hear.

She shifted position and smiled as her behind knocked some of the keys in a very undignified way.

She gave a small laugh. 'I guess my derrière doesn't have the same quality as you.'

But Javier was watching her as if he was entranced. She lifted one hand to his cheek. 'I'm glad that you shared it with me. You have no idea how much I've missed you. How many times I've wanted to phone or text you. Sometimes just to talk about the way things ended that morning between us, and how it always felt so wrong. And other times about work stuff—there were a million occasions I could have discussed patients with you. I would have loved your opinion on—' she gave him a cheeky smile and then bent down and whispered in his ear '—you know, just so you could tell me that I was right.'

He leaned his head further into her hand. 'Let's not lose this again, Caitlin. Promise me we are always going to be friends. In future, we will always be able to pick up the phone to each other.'

Her stomach gave an uneasy lurch. She was thinking about Natalia's impending surgery. There was always a chance it might not be successful. There was also the risk that something unexpected could happen. All of sudden, she didn't want to do that surgery.

She didn't want to be the person who had to tell Javier something had gone wrong and break his heart. She breathed in deeply. She couldn't admit that. She couldn't say that out loud. And she didn't want to. She didn't want to spoil this moment or this connection.

She leaned forward and kissed him. 'You will always be the first person I want to phone, Javier.'

He stood up, putting his hands on the silk of her dress and lifting her up onto the piano. She didn't care about the sounds coming from the angry keys as body parts pushed against them. All she cared about was the man she was kissing.

She pushed his tuxedo jacket from his shoulders, letting it fall carelessly on the floor. Her hands went to the white shirt, and she undid the buttons like the expert surgeon she was.

His hands pushed her silk dress up past her

thighs and pulled her closer. This room was private. They wouldn't be disturbed.

'You were right,' she agreed as his hand traced down the middle of her body, making her catch her breath. 'This has been the perfect date.'

His head lifted and he gave her a wicked grin. 'And it's not finished yet.'

CHAPTER SEVEN

'WHAT'S WRONG WITH the echo?'

Caitlin was standing with her arms crossed in the doorway, listening to Javier question one of their interns.

It didn't matter that it was the middle of the night. Every scan was a teaching opportunity, and Javier was a great teacher.

She stood back, watching someone else take on the role that usually fell to her. It was actually nice sharing the load. Their teaching styles were slightly different. Caitlin liked to question students, see what she could pull from the back of their brain and sometimes make them puzzle their way to the answer.

Javier started with basics. He then cut to the chase and explained everything they needed to know. But they shouldn't get complacent, because the next time a similar case appeared he would expect them to have learned, revised and remembered. The mixture of both techniques seemed to be working well with the junior doctors that they were training and mentoring.

This intern was promising, pointing out the slight inflammation showing on the scan and asking a few pertinent questions. This patient had endocarditis—inflammation of the heart muscle, in this case caused by a dental procedure. It was unusual, and she was glad they'd picked it up. The condition was entirely treatable and catching it quickly would likely stop the possibility of long-term damage.

When Javier had finished, he glanced in her direction as his page sounded. He gave a thoughtful nod. 'Want to join me in the ER?' he asked.

She nodded as they walked along the corridor. 'It's a teenage patient,' he said. 'They just want a review before deciding if they send him on to Madrid.'

Caitlin nodded. The hospital in Barcelona didn't have a paediatric cardiothoracic surgeon, and some of their patients were referred on.

'Teenagers are the most tricky,' she said as they reached the stairs. 'It really depends on their size, weight and cardiac history.'

'You are fine dealing with teenagers?'

She nodded. 'Mostly. I can always dial in Josef if I need a second opinion. He's a paediatric cardiothoracic surgeon in Madrid who has a consultation contract with St Aelina's. And he's great; day or night, if I give him a call, he always makes himself available.'

'What about the younger children?'

She shook her head as they descended the stairs. 'No, too small for my big hands,' she joked as she held them up. 'And I don't go near the neonates at all. Was it Santiago who paged you?'

Javier nodded.

'He's our most experienced paediatrician. What I like most about him is that he doesn't hesitate to ask another specialist for an opinion. Whether it's cardiac, oncology, urology, renal. I respect that. He knows that we're mainly adult doctors, but he seems to value having a conversation with a specialist in whatever area the child presents with.'

Javier held open the door at the bottom of the stairs. 'My living nightmare would be to be a generalist—as is expected of many of the paediatricians. You can't possibly hope to know everything about every condition.' He gave an appreciative nod. 'I like that he asks questions, even if it is the middle of the night.'

They glanced at the whiteboard to find which patient Santiago García was with. It was a fourteen-year-old boy. Caitlin found the cubicle easily and pulled back the curtains slightly. 'Santiago, hi—all right to come in?'

The dark-haired doctor gave a broad smile and a nod and Caitlin slipped behind the curtain. 'Santiago, this is Javier Torres. He holds the same role as I do, and normally works in Madrid. He's here for a few weeks helping out and he's on call tonight, so he got your page.'

Santiago didn't hesitate to hold out his hand and shake Javier's hand. 'Pleasure to meet you. Thanks for coming.' He turned to the teenager on the bed. 'Two for the price of one,' he said with a smile. 'These are the guys I told you would come and take a look at your chest X-ray for me and listen to your heart. Are you okay with that?'

The teenage boy nodded. He had sandy-coloured hair and blue eyes. 'Joel is fourteen and plays football. Tonight, at a game, he felt short of breath and had some chest pain as he was playing. His coach drove him here—his father has taken his younger sister to relatives for the night. He'll be back shortly.'

Caitlin and Javier both nodded. Javier picked up an ECG that had been taken earlier, and Caitlin pressed the button on the monitor to recheck the blood pressure, which was higher than it should be.

The tiny fleeting glance from Santiago told Caitlin all she needed to know. He was worried. As the on-call paediatrician, Santiago would see lots of kids in the ER overnight, and Caitlin was happy to help out a friend. When she'd first arrived in Barcelona he'd been welcoming and happy to help her get settled. They'd formed a lasting friendship that had also grown into professional respect as they'd worked together the last few years. Caitlin had no doubt. If she ever had kids, Santiago was the guy she would want to be their paediatrician.

Javier had walked around to the other side of the trolley. 'Joel, tell me what happened this evening.'

'I was playing football. We'd been playing for around thirty minutes and I was feeling a bit out of breath.'

'Has that happened before?'

Joel shifted uncomfortably on the hospital trolley. 'Maybe, well…more so in the last few months.'

'What do you do when you feel out of breath?' asked Caitlin, knowing what the answer would likely be.

Joel frowned. 'Well, it's football, you're supposed to be out of breath, so I just push through.'

She could tell that Santiago already had the same suspicions that she had—that was why he'd called them.

Javier continued, 'And what happened next?'

'My chest started to feel tight. As if something was pressing on it. Then I felt like I'd been punched, so I had to stop.' The teenager looked embarrassed. 'Coach made a fuss, stopped the game and made me sit out for a bit. When I still had the heavy feeling in my chest he brought me here. But it's nothing, isn't it? Can I play football again tomorrow? We have a school game.'

Javier gave him a cautious smile. 'How is your chest pain now?'

Again, Joel shifted. 'It's still there,' he admitted, 'but just a bit.'

'Can I have a listen to your chest?' asked Javier.

Joel nodded and straightened up in the bed. Caitlin waited while Javier listened. When he sat Joel forward to listen to his back, he gave her a nod and she put her stethoscope to her ears and listened to Joel's chest too.

A technician appeared, wheeling in the cardiac echo machine. Caitlin gave Santiago a grateful smile. He'd known exactly what they would need.

'Are you happy for me to continue?' asked Javier.

Caitlin nodded, pleased by his acknowledgement. He didn't need to do that, but the fact that he had made her feel warm all over. Javier lifted the transducer and explained what he was doing to Joel. Caitlin watched the screen and saw exactly what she'd expected to.

Santiago's tablet gave a ping and he turned it towards her. 'Chest X-ray is ready.'

She took the tablet for a few minutes and gave a nod.

Javier was talking football to Joel. Within a few moments the two of them were conversing in rapid Spanish, arguing good-naturedly over the best team and the most skilful player. The Spanish was so fast that even though she'd lived here for a few years she still struggled to follow it.

Once he'd finished the echo, he wiped Joel's chest clean. 'I'm going to see if your *papá* has got back yet,' he said, giving Santiago and Caitlin a quick look. 'We'll be back in a few minutes.'

Joel lay back on the trolley and picked up his phone, instantly scrolling.

The three doctors walked a little further down the corridor to the nurses' station.

'What do you think?' asked Santiago.

'The same as you do,' said Javier. He turned to Caitlin. 'Agreed?'

She nodded. 'It looks like he's had Kawasaki disease in the past. I've checked his notes and there's no mention of it. But he did have an ER visit as a three-year-old with a high temperature and viral infection.'

The other two groaned. Javier had his hands on his hips and shook his head. 'So, because it's been missed and untreated, we're just about to break this teenager's heart about when he can play football again. The damage is extensive. One of his coronary arteries is partially blocked and I think we need further studies on his valves.'

'His blood pressure is too high.' Caitlin was shaking her head. 'Give me a buzz when his blood work is back. If it's good, let's get him started on an ACE inhibitor, and consider a calcium channel blocker too.'

Santiago gave a serious nod. He checked with one of the nursing staff. 'Is Joel's father back yet?'

She shook her head. 'There's a road traffic accident. He's stuck in traffic but will be here shortly.'

'I'll speak to him alongside you,' Caitlin said to Santiago. 'I'm happy to wait around until he gets here.'

Santiago turned to Javier. 'You and Joel seemed to hit it off. Do you mind keeping him company while we talk to his *papá*?'

'Absolutely. I'll prepare him a little for what is coming next.' He gave Caitlin a regretful glance then walked back down to the cubicle.

Santiago turned to face her. 'Want to fill me in?'

She started, surprised by the sudden turn in conversation. 'What do you mean?'

'We're friends, right?'

She could feel blood rushing to her cheeks and wished she had a way to stop it. 'Right,' she replied cautiously.

He gave her a knowing smile. 'So, I called Javier down for a consult and you came too. And not because you're supervising or don't trust him. The two of you are joined at the hip. Should I buy a hat?'

She batted his arm. 'Stop it. You're being ridiculous. We're...old friends.'

Santiago laughed. 'Is that what we're calling it now?' He stared down the now empty corridor. 'Well, I like him. He's switched on. Seems good at his job. He's from Madrid?'

Caitlin nodded, knowing she could trust Santiago with a few details. 'His sister is upstairs. I'm about to perform surgery on her and he's worried, so he came along. He's here for a few weeks.'

'Is that all? What a shame.'

Something washed over Caitlin. The reminder that time was short.

'There's something about him,' said Santiago, his brow creased. 'I feel as if I recognise him.'

'Do you?'

Santiago looked thoughtful. 'Maybe we were at the same medical school.'

Caitlin shook her head. 'He trained with me in London.'

Santiago's eyebrows shot up. 'So, you are old friends.'

She gave him a nod. 'Of course. I told you.' A nurse gave them a wave and she was glad of the interruption. 'Looks like Joel's *papá* is here. Shall we go and have a chat?'

Santiago's face was serious again, his mind straight back to the situation. 'Absolutely, let's go.'

Javier was surprised by how much he liked this place. Hospitals were hospitals. But every hospital had a vibe. And not all of them were good. But St Aelina's was a combination of all the things he liked. Busy, sometimes frantic, with committed, friendly staff. No wonder Caitlin had settled in so well here.

He liked the people too. He'd heard a few of the staff discussing Santiago. He was well respected. He'd heard the same about some of the other staff he was working with. It gave him confidence in the place his sister would be operated on.

Of course, the most important person in that equation was the surgeon. And he'd always had confidence in Caitlin. If he were lying on a trolley, it would be Caitlin he'd want to operate on him, so of course he'd recommended her for his sister.

Natalia was sleeping right now. Thank goodness. She hadn't been sleeping well at night and it was important she was well rested for her surgery.

His mother had been on the phone earlier, asking about his sister, then telling him she'd email with a list of priorities that needed to be dealt with on the estate. He felt like the naughty schoolboy who hadn't done his homework. There was no point trying to tell his mother that he was doing a full-time job here, overseeing his sister's care, catching up on referrals or reviews for his own patients back in Madrid and spending every other waking moment thinking about Caitlin. The estate didn't feature in his thoughts. Not really. Except for hanging in the background like a dark thundercloud.

He hated that he felt that way about the childhood home that was full of such good memories, and the place and business he knew that the rest of the family adored.

Maybe it was just because he was the only son. The new Conde. The expectations had been there from birth. There had been no opportunity for Javier to decide what he wanted to do with his life. In a way he'd been lucky that his mother and father had allowed him his dream of going to medical school and training as a doctor. They could easily have refused—or made his life difficult.

But his father had been well. The old Conde had expected to live for much longer than he had. He'd thought there would be plenty of time to bring his son back into his role to fulfil his family responsibilities. Unfortunately, life had decided to go a different way.

Javier sat down in a comfortable chair in Natalia's darkened room, lifting his tablet and connecting to his emails. He tried to read them—he really did. But his brain just couldn't focus. He was thinking of the young man down in the ER, and the expression on his face when Javier had gently told him that things might be more serious and taken him through a brief biology lesson of the heart and blood vessels. He was thinking what the future might hold for that young man.

A hand appeared on his shoulder and he jumped. 'Hey,' said Caitlin softly. 'Thought I might find you here. How about some company?'

He stood up and she slipped her hand into his and they walked back along the corridor to her office.

Javier had learned quickly that it was really her second home. She had a whole wardrobe in there, a fold-down bed, a functioning bathroom and a secret stash of chocolate. It was so Caitlin.

She pulled out her ponytail band and shook

out her hair. She pressed the button to make her sofa bed fold down, which Javier loved.

'Isn't technology amazing?'

'Yes,' she agreed, flopping down onto the bed. 'Especially when it does this for me.'

He laughed and moved next to her, stretching his legs out.

'We still have another four hours to work.'

She sighed and turned onto her side, wrapping one arm and one leg over him. 'Okay then, any objections if I do it like this?'

Heat swept over him, just like any time he was around Caitlin. Everything about this seemed so right. This—here—felt like a perfect moment for him.

If an asteroid hit the planet right now and this was his last memory, this was exactly where he wanted to be, and who he wanted to be with.

He hated that this was temporary. He hated that he could never dream of asking Caitlin to give up her career and job and come with him back to the estate. It was his duty, not hers. And in his head he could already see that neither of them would be happy.

But he would never ask her to do that anyway. He would never ask Caitlin to give up her dreams for him. He wouldn't dare. The

Glasgow girl would probably kill him mid-sentence, and that made him smile. She could be fierce when she wanted to be.

Caitlin hid things well. He knew the relationship with her parents wasn't good. She'd opened up a little more about that, and it was a first. He'd always known they weren't particularly interested in Caitlin, and that amazed him. They had a wonderful daughter, intelligent, compassionate, and they barely noticed. It made him angry. But he knew his anger wouldn't help Caitlin.

He also knew that he'd lived a privileged life. Deprivation had never touched the early part of Javier's life. But being a doctor had brought him a much better understanding that where you lived and having limited choices could all affect a person's health. Caitlin had spoken briefly about the area in Glasgow she'd grown up in. He knew she had worked really hard to get a scholarship to go to medical school in London. He'd also helped her hide the fact she'd needed a job in order to eat at medical school. She hadn't wanted or asked for his help—in fact, he'd seen the panic in her eyes when he'd walked into the book-shop and realised she was working there. It had taken all her angry strength to ask him to keep her job a secret, something he'd willingly agreed to. Of course, he'd had the means to offer her financial support instead of keeping her secret. But he'd known straight away that her pride wouldn't let her accept that from him, and he'd admired her for it. Even on their date, when he'd arranged to get some dresses for her, he'd been part worried she would turn them down. Sure enough, everything but the one she'd worn had been left with instructions for them to be returned, but at least she'd accepted the gift in the spirit it had been intended.

'Are you ready for Wednesday?' he asked.

She lifted her head and kissed him on the lips. Wednesday was Natalia's surgery. Tonight was their last night shift together. Caitlin was swapping back to days to perform Natalia's surgery in four days' time.

He trusted her. He trusted Caitlin implicitly. But that didn't stop the deep-seated worries that something could go wrong for his sister.

Her fingers ran through his hair. 'Of course I'm ready. Am I nervous? Of course I am. Because this is your sister. You love her. She's my friend. I want the best outcome in the world for her, and I hope I can make that happen. But we're surgeons, Javier. We have to expect the unexpected. But I promise you I will do my absolute best to make sure everything goes exactly the way it should.'

Her green eyes were staring straight at him, full of emotion and sincerity. It filled his heart with joy, and a tiny bit of dread. He knew about surgery. And if something went wrong would he feel differently about Caitlin? Probably. And that made him shallow.

If the roles were reversed and Caitlin had a brother he was about to operate on, how would he feel? Terrified would be the short answer. Terrified if things went wrong, how it would impact on the relationship with someone that he loved.

Loved. He'd always loved her, but in a different way. He was loyal to his friends. Always had been. But things had changed between them. Even after that night they'd spent together, when his mind had been a reckless jumble, he'd known deep down how he'd felt about her.

When she'd acted as if their night together had been nothing—just a build-up of sexual tension between them rather than something more deep-seated—he'd been devastated.

But, as a typical man, he'd acted with bravado instead of asking her to sit down and talk.

He didn't doubt for a single second that Caitlin would do her absolute best for Natalia. That was why he'd brought Natalia here. He'd brought her to the best surgeon that he knew, and someone he trusted completely. So much was at risk.

He knew that every family member felt like this. Even for the most basic procedure in the world, every parent, every sibling or every child had that moment of absolute fear when a loved one disappeared through the theatre doors. It was normal. It was natural. And he'd had this conversation a hundred times with family members to let them know their feelings were entirely normal. They weren't irrational. They weren't overthinking things. They were human.

Javier's problem was that he was usually on the other side of the theatre doors. He was usually the one with the words of wisdom and reassurance rather than the person standing at the other side. He didn't like this position.

He hated feeling as if there were things he couldn't control. And now it seemed as if there was so much around him he couldn't control. The surgery for his sister. His future as a surgeon. His relationship with Caitlin. So much that could all change in a heartbeat. Javier had never had so much uncertainty in his life. It made him want to cling on all the harder.

Tonight, as he lay in his perfect place with Caitlin, he could almost hear the clock ticking down slowly, calling time on their relationship.

He wished he'd spent the last few years with her. Even if it would still have come to this eventual outcome, he would have had a few years' worth of memories to take him into the next stage of his life.

Reflecting now was easy. He'd tried hard to love Elisabeth, but now he could see it would never have worked. Not when he'd always feel this way about Caitlin. He would never have been able to throw his heart and soul into another relationship. Not when his heart belonged to another.

As guilt pricked at him, he wondered how they should leave things. He wanted her to be happy. He wanted Caitlin to be free to lead the life she should, to find love, to get married and have a family if she chose to. He didn't want her to feel like he currently did—that their connection would never leave him, and he could never really love someone else.

Carrying those feelings was a definite burden. It didn't matter to him what came next. His life would be at the family estate; their plans for the future would never be compatible. Maybe his mother would try and matchmake again? Maybe he would meet someone who, for reasons of their own, would be happy to settle and just live a comfortable, companionable life.

He shuddered. What a thought.

'What's wrong?' asked Caitlin. Her fingers traced down his forehead to the tip of his nose, her touch as light as a feather.

'Nothing,' he said, pushing everything else away. 'I just know that after all of this I will miss you.'

Sadness flooded her eyes. She gave a smile. 'But we'll have this,' she said. 'This time together, and these moments.' She took a deep breath. 'And I can't be sad about that. I can't be sad about this.'

'Me neither,' he agreed as he pulled her even closer, then he laughed. 'So, our memories will be of a fold-down bed in an office in St Aelina's. Instead of in a luxury hotel with Egyptian cotton and a four-poster bed.'

'Oh, we can still make memories there too,' she whispered.

She slid on top of him. 'And you know what they say, practice makes perfect.' And she sealed those words with another kiss.

CHAPTER EIGHT

THE PAEDIATRIC CARDIOTHORACIC surgeon on the teleconference gave a sincere smile. 'I absolutely agree this is the way to proceed. Thank you for agreeing to take on this case.'

Javier gave a nod. 'No problem. I'll come back to you once the procedure is complete.'

He cut the call and turned to Caitlin. 'Anything you want to raise?'

She shook her head. 'I'm fine with everything that was discussed. Joel is almost the size of a regular adult. I'm hopeful that the angioplasty will be straightforward.'

Javier nodded. It wasn't the first time he'd done the procedure on a teenager, and Joel seemed to have struck up a rapport with him and they all agreed that was beneficial for the person performing his procedure.

For Javier it was something he did on a regular basis. The anatomy and physiology would be the same, just the age of the patient would be different.

'Do you want to assist?' he asked Caitlin. He didn't have to worry about her being offended by him asking. She nodded straight away. She was supposed to be off today, to give herself a little rest before Natalia's surgery, but Caitlin was, like him, always ready to work when asked.

He felt a pang of dread. This had been his way of life for so long. What would happen when he couldn't do this any more? Could he really find life fulfilling at the estate? He hated how he felt inside right now.

Javier tried to push it all to one side. He had a teenage boy to concentrate on. Joel's life had already changed irrevocably. It was up to him to attempt to control the damage and minimise the impact on Joel's life.

He waited while Joel was moved into the pre-op room and went to stand alongside him, asking him and his *papá* if they had any questions before they started, and letting Bill, the anaesthetist, explain how he would make sure that Joel was comfortable and wouldn't feel anything untoward during the procedure. He gave Joel some mild sedation and they waited for it to take effect.

Caitlin scrubbed up alongside Javier and then stood to one side as Joel was wheeled into the theatre.

Everything was in place. The staff gave him nods that they were ready to start and Javier turned to Joel. 'We're ready to start. At any point if you have a question, just ask. If you don't feel well at any stage, tell us too. Any discomfort at all, let Bill know and we'll stop.' Javier paused. All Joel's initial nonchalance and bravado had clearly been left at the door. 'I know this is scary. But it won't take long, and I've done dozens of these procedures. If this works the way it should, the blood flow to your heart will improve and you shouldn't have some of the symptoms you've been experiencing.'

Joel gave a nod, but he looked as if he could burst into tears at any second.

Javier nodded to someone to push a stool in behind him and he sat down at the edge of the operating table. 'Okay, let's talk for a while. Let's dream team. Pick your first player.'

Caitlin was smiling under her mask. Javier didn't care about theatre times. He didn't care about being the most prolific surgeon. What he did care about was this fourteen-year-old on the operating table.

And what she loved most about her workplace was the fact that everyone got it. No one sighed…no one rolled their eyes. She could sense them all smiling behind their masks too. Fifteen minutes later, Javier and Joel were still arguing over their teams and players. It was actually beautiful to watch.

When Javier finally moved into position, Joel was clearly much more relaxed. When Javier inserted the thin flexible catheter into his femoral artery via a small incision in his groin, Joel only flinched for a second.

Caitlin watched the screen as the catheter was guided up Joel's artery. The narrowing was clearly evident as they reached the blockage. 'Now,' Javier instructed Caitlin and she injected the contrast dye through the catheter. The blockage was even more pronounced than they'd initially thought.

This boy had been running around a football park with almost blocked arteries. They knew exactly what might have happened.

'Okay?' checked Javier. Sometimes when the dye was inserted, patients could feel lightheaded or nauseous. But Joel was lying with his eyes closed and just nodded his head.

'Fine,' he murmured.

Javier was skilful. Now the blockage was clearly identified, he threaded the guidewire inside the catheter across the narrowed area. Next, a long thin tube was inserted. It had an uninflated balloon at one end and was guided to the blocked area.

Once Javier was sure it was exactly in position, he inflated the balloon, flattening the plaque within the artery and inserting a stent into place to ensure the artery stayed open. He kept talking quietly and steadily to Joel the whole time.

It was clear he had no idea if the sedation had taken hold of Joel and the young man had actually fallen asleep, or if Joel was keeping his eyes closed to try and relax during the procedure. What Caitlin absolutely knew for sure was that Joel was central to every single thing that Javier was doing right now. He was the focus of his entire world.

Part of her crumbled inside at the irony of all this. Javier Torres was a spectacular doctor. He was so talented, and the thought of him giving all this up to run a vineyard and ancestral estate just seemed like such a waste.

She knew he was a Count. She didn't really understand the aristocracy side of all this because it had never been a world that she'd moved in. But surgery was a world that she did move in. And right now she wanted to shout on behalf of all cardiothoracic surgeons about how ridiculous this all was. How many students could he train? How many lives could he save? What on earth could he use skills like this for in a vineyard?

More importantly, how many situations like this would be lost? She already knew that this fourteen-year-old boy would never forget Javier Torres. He would remember this whole experience based on the relationship that Javier had established with him. The jokes, the trust, this whole thing would be etched in his brain.

And Caitlin wanted to sit in a corner and cry for all those people who wouldn't get the chance to meet this wonderful doctor doing the job he'd clearly been born to do.

Life just seemed so unfair right now, and that was without throwing herself into the equation. Anger bubbled up inside her. She was glad she still had a mask on and that her expression was hidden.

Javier was still working away diligently. He removed the catheter and applied a collagen plug to help seal the wound, his eyes flicking to the monitors at the end of the table which showed Joel's blood pressure and heart rate.

He put a wound pad over the insertion point and moved up to the top of the table. 'Joel, that's us finished. You did absolutely great. I'm going to send you back up to the ward to rest, then I'll come and speak to you later about what happens next.'

Joel's eyes flickered open for a few seconds and he nodded. Javier gave Joel's hand a tap. 'I'll go and speak to your *papá* now. All I need you to do is rest. And I don't want you to get up for a few hours. So do what the nursing staff tell you.'

Bill, the anaesthetist, gave Javier and Caitlin a nod and walked alongside the trolley as it was wheeled out to the post-op room.

Javier pulled off his pale green surgical hat and then his gloves and gown, breathing a big sigh of relief.

He gave a few instructions to one of the nurses and Caitlin moved alongside him.

'You did great,' she said, unable to hide the admiration in her voice.

He looked sideways at her as he started washing his hands again. 'Thanks. It was a simple procedure. I just hope it will make the difference it needs to for Joel's life. We're just going to have to wait and see. That's the hardest part of this job.'

No. It wasn't. The hardest part of this job was watching a friend walk away from the job they should keep doing for ever.

Every cell in her body wanted to take him away from here, drag him to the diner—or his hotel—across the road, and sit him down and talk him out of all this.

But she also knew that she couldn't. She'd absolutely no right to do that at all. The horrible fact was that Caitlin McKenzie knew exactly the kind of person that Javier Torres had been for six years of her life. What little she knew of him now told her that in principle he hadn't really changed.

Javier Torres took responsibility seriously. She knew that ultimately he would do what he thought was best. And he'd already told her what that was. He would take over the estate, as his parents had expected him to do, and to relieve the pressure on his sister. To let his sister make a full recovery after her surgery and possibly help her prepare for a different future. He would take the place that was his birthright.

Count Javier. His title would have already changed to the Count of Maravilla. His mother's title at this stage was honorary. If Javier married, then his new wife would be the Countess.

Caitlin had looked up the word *maravilla*. It could mean two things. One was marigold; the other was wonder. The Count of Wonder. She smiled again. Her brain had conjured a hundred different ways that Javier could be a Count of Wonder. Every single one of them would be entirely censored.

'What's wrong?' he said, nudging her with his elbow before drying his hands.

She shook her head. She couldn't have this conversation with him. She stared into those big, sincere brown eyes. This was why she thought so much of him. Because he was entirely *this* man.

She couldn't ask him not to do what he considered his duty. Just like he would never ask her to give up what she loved.

That struck her heart. Did he feel as deeply as she did?

Maybe it just suited her to think so, but in her heart she felt that he did. She knew that he wouldn't ask her to join him at his side to run the estate. He would never ask her to give up the life she'd fought so hard for. And she was glad. Because she wouldn't want to make that decision. She wouldn't want to choose between the two big loves of her life. He would choose for her. He wouldn't put her in that position.

'You okay?' he asked. She'd still been staring at him. Lost in the thoughts in her head.

She slipped her arm into his. 'Once you've finished talking to Joel's *papá*, let's take an hour out. Let's get changed and go and get a coffee and some cake at a café somewhere.'

He gave her a curious stare then his handsome face broke into a smile. 'Absolutely.'

She wanted to get some space. Out of here. Away from everything. Away from their past, and away from their future. Because, for the here and now, Javier Torres was still hers. And, no matter what else was going on around them, she was going to hold onto that for as long as she possibly could.

CHAPTER NINE

IT WAS THE morning of surgery and Caitlin was eerily calm. She'd hoped to spend last night with Javier. But the night had turned into a disaster, with both of them being called to separate theatres in the early hours.

As much as she'd wanted to spend every second with him, they'd reluctantly parted at three a.m. They had to. They both knew that Caitlin needed to sleep if she were to perform Natalia's surgery in the morning.

As it was, she'd pushed the surgery back from eight a.m. to ten a.m., thanks to another colleague who was always happy to take an earlier slot. It meant in theory she should have had enough rest, but her sleep had been restless and she'd tossed and turned.

It actually wasn't the thought of the surgery that had her so concerned. She was confident in the procedures and her techniques. It was the 'what came next' that made her stomach churn over and over.

She did all her usual rituals. Her lucky surgical hat. Her favourite surgical scrubs. A pair of coloured flat theatre shoes.

She had a coffee and ate a slice of toast.

She greeted all her theatre staff the way she normally did, then spent ten minutes re-checking all test results, plus the bloods from Natalia that had been taken that morning.

She was joined by the surgical staff who would be assisting—clearly Javier was not allowed in the theatre—then she went to meet Natalia in the pre-op room. The anaesthetist, Andreas, was already with her and chatting easily. 'Morning, Natalia, apologies about the late start.'

'It's fine; Javier explained. He slept in the chair in my room last night.'

Of course he had. She wouldn't have expected any different.

'Would you like me to go over things with you again this morning?'

Natalia shook her head. 'No, thanks. I just want to get this over with. I want to wake up later today, with you standing next to me saying everything went fine, and knowing that my brother will finally breathe again.'

Caitlin reached over and took Natalia's hand. 'We will talk later, and let's go with your prediction. Because that's what I want too.'

Natalia squeezed her hand and Caitlin could see the tears in her eyes. 'Thank you,' she whispered, her voice breaking. 'And if anything...'

Caitlin shook her own head and put a finger to her lips. 'Don't. I have a rule that none of my patients are allowed to talk like that.'

Natalia gave a weak smile. 'Well, I've always been a rule-breaker. Promise to look after my brother.'

It was like a vice gripping Caitlin's heart and squeezing tight. She couldn't even let her thoughts move into that space at all. There was no room for thoughts like those.

She pasted a smile on her face. 'Natalia, I'll see you later today. Just like we planned.' She gave her a smile before walking back through to the theatre and starting to scrub.

She concentrated on her hands, the most important part of her body right now. Staff spoke to her as they moved around her. She was conscious of the trolley being wheeled in and Natalia being moved over to the operating table. As she finished scrubbing and pulled on her gloves, one of the nurses came up and tied her mask into place for her.

She waited until Andreas gave her the nod that he and the patient were ready for her before she nodded to her team to approach the table. For the procedure today, Caitlin would have to do the most traditional of incisions. Natalia would also need to go on cardiopulmonary bypass to stop her heart beating and allow the replacement of the valves to be carried out. There were risks for every part of the procedure and Caitlin was focused. This was more than her A game.

There was a viewing gallery above this theatre. She wondered if any other doctors would be watching today. The gallery had floor-to-ceiling windows, and screens so that the meticulous detail of whatever operation was being performed could be captured by the cameras in the theatre. It was a wonderful way for other surgeons to learn. Numbers in the actual theatre had to be kept to a minimum and this way the learning was shared with everyone.

But Caitlin would not raise her head. She would not look. She would tell herself that Javier was not there watching her. She didn't need that extra pressure and her whole focus had to be on Natalia. She sucked in a deep breath and steadied her nerves.

Her colleague next to her started the procedures for bypass. They were a meticulous practitioner and Caitlin was lucky to work alongside them. When things were ready for her part, she swabbed her area for incision and ensured that Natalia was draped appropriately. She made the large chest incision, spreading the ribcage, allowing the heart to be exposed, then inserted the cannula into the right atrium to remove blood, and into the ascending aorta to return the blood to Natalia's system.

As soon as the cardiopulmonary bypass started, a theatre auxiliary started the clock.

When things were stable, Caitlin began her part of the procedure, removing and replacing the two damaged heart valves. Both were worse than she'd feared and she absolutely knew that they'd made the right decision bringing Natalia in for surgery.

Time ticked past slowly. At one point a staff member brought her something to drink through a straw. She took a few minutes to sit down on a stool as the anaesthetist changed some of the drugs he was administering and wanted to monitor things closely.

Both of her surgical assistants were clearly nervous. They knew that this was Javier's sister and both were on the cardiothoracic training programme in Spain. It was inevitable that they might meet him at some stage. She'd already been told good-humouredly by another staff member that one had been heard being sick in the changing rooms.

The sense of humour of theatre staff was unique, to say the least, and Caitlin had only enquired if the staff member was fit enough to be on duty. Both were doing well and she would give them good write-ups after their debriefing later today.

She arched her back. The temperature in the theatre was carefully controlled—particularly during a bypass procedure. It was always slightly cool, and Caitlin could feel it through the thin theatre gown on her arms, which she was pretty sure were covered in goosebumps.

As she put the final stitch in place, every muscle and bone in her body ached. She wanted to cry. She wanted to cry with relief that the surgery had gone well. She wanted to cry for Javier that he would now be able to shake off the dark cloud hanging over his head.

She wanted to cry for herself because she

knew what came next. But Caitlin was professional to the core. Always had been, and always would be.

She lifted her head to address the staff. 'And…we're done. Thank you everyone; your hard work and attention to detail is much appreciated.'

Andreas moved around. The immediate recovery from anaesthetic was his domain.

There was a noise above her, and Caitlin looked up. She'd refused to lift her head during the surgery, wondering if Javier would be in the viewing gallery. He was leaning against the glass, looking down at her with an expression she'd never seen before. Even from here she could see a tear rolling down one cheek.

He pressed both hands into a prayer position and mouthed the word *gracias* to her.

She knew he wouldn't have come into the viewing gallery until surgery was underway, to preserve his sister's dignity. She knew he would have turned his head away as the final stitches to her chest wall were being inserted.

She gave him a nod and walked over to the waste bin to strip off her theatre garb. Once she'd washed up, she went through to post-op where Andreas and a range of other staff were overseeing the care. Natalia's vitals were steady.

She gave a few last-minute instructions and let the staff know she had her page if they needed her, before heading out of the door.

Javier was in the corridor outside the exit from Theatre. Caitlin thought for around ten seconds before opening the door to Recovery and letting him through.

The gratitude in his eyes was more than she required. The staff were familiar with him now, and moved aside to let him look at his sister, hold her hand, stroke her hair and kiss her forehead.

Caitlin stayed for the next six hours, knowing they were vital, wanting to be on hand if Natalia threw off newly formed clots, or started bleeding from any of her wound sites. The blood's ability to clot could be affected in many ways due to the surgery type, the bypass or the anaesthesia, and these first few hours were crucial. Javier sat patiently on the other side of Natalia's bed, barely speaking. He didn't need to. His eyes were flitting between every syringe driver, every pump and the constant changes on the cardiac monitor, showing heart rhythm, blood pressure and oxygen saturation.

When she was eventually satisfied the most important hours had passed, she finally stood up and stretched out her back.

When he followed her back outside his relief was palpable. 'Thank you,' he said.

She couldn't help the wave of sadness washing over her. The surgery was done. Javier would be leaving.

She held out her hand to him, her voice cracking. 'Time to say goodbye,' she whispered as he took her hand in his.

It was ridiculous. He knew it was. But it felt as though the weight of a thousand elephants sitting on his chest was finally gone.

They walked through the hospital corridors, saying hello to a few colleagues as they passed. More than a few glanced at their clasped hands. He could see the way people were looking at Caitlin with renewed interest. He guessed she usually didn't give them much to gossip about. They'd been mainly on nights together, so it was likely their closeness had been missed by some. But now, walking down the corridors hand in hand, it was like a huge flag waving. Caitlin didn't seem the slightest bit worried.

His mind naturally went back to how dif-

ferent she'd been twelve years ago after they'd
spent the night together. Then, she'd seemed
unsure and full of regret, brushing off their
night together as if it had meant nothing.
Today, she seemed sure about what she was
doing.

They reached his hotel room quickly. And
while Javier might have wanted to strip his
clothes off in seconds, this was goodbye and
he wanted to take things slowly.

He cupped Caitlin's face in his hands and
whispered, 'I'm never going to be sorry about
this. I'm going to take the best memories of
us with me. You're always going to have a
piece of my heart, Cait.'

She blinked, her eyes filling with tears, and
pulled him close to her so the full length of
their bodies was touching. She held him there,
letting them both feel the heat of each other
through their thin scrubs. He would remember this too. Remember the way the curves
of her body fitted against his. Like perfect
pieces of a jigsaw puzzle.

They moved over to the bed and made love
for a final time. His emotions were wrought.

As they lay in bed with the bright sun
streaming through the chinks in the curtains,
he ran one finger along the curve of her hip.

He wanted to make a million suggestions. That she should visit him. Holiday at the estate. Meet up every few months or so. But what would that do to Caitlin?

Whilst it might suit Javier, ultimately it wouldn't let Caitlin live the life she should. It would always come down to the question of her not being able to live full-time with him on the estate, and their life being a transient one.

It wouldn't help either of them. He knew this should be it. Their final goodbye. Yes, they could be friends. But from a distance. This woman had more of his heart than she really knew. And it wouldn't do any good to tell her that. She had to be free to move on and meet someone else. Someone who could be by her side as her career flourished.

For all he knew, she might intend to eventually go back to Scotland. He didn't doubt that other hospitals in other countries would approach her and try to poach her from her current post. Cardiothoracic surgery was such a specialist area. He was absolutely sure that his own hospital in Madrid would make her an offer once he handed in his notice.

'I will miss you,' he said softly. 'And I will always treasure our time together.'

Her auburn hair was spread out across the white sheets and he picked up a tress and wound it around his finger. 'Every little part of it.'

Caitlin closed her eyes for a second, then moved and kissed him on the forehead. 'I have to move. I have to get back. I have a very important patient to review.'

He nodded. He'd known this. And he was absolutely determined to make sure that this goodbye wasn't like the last.

He swung his legs around, ignoring the wrench in his stomach at breaking away from her warm skin. He walked into the bathroom and flicked on the shower. He could hear Caitlin moving around too. A few seconds later there was the sound of the shower in the other room.

They had to keep everything in check. It was no good being overemotional or making promises they would both eventually break.

This time it really was goodbye.

Caitlin blasted her hair with the dryer in the room to take the dampness out of it, then twisted it in a knot at the back of her neck and pulled on her scrubs.

She was finding it hard to keep things together. A few seconds ago she'd wanted to hand in her notice and move to the country. A minute before that she'd been trying to work out how she could commute to the estate.

It was hopeless. And they both knew it. But saying goodbye was harder than she'd ever imagined. Her heart was truly broken.

It had to be this way, but it didn't make things any easier.

Her phone buzzed and she picked it up, reading the text and swiping it away. Her eyes went automatically to her feed and she flicked through a few headlines. None meant much to her. She didn't really watch the news. But a photo caught her eye and she stopped dead.

Javier. A photo of Javier was in the news. Along with the name of her hospital.

There was even a slightly blurred picture, clearly taken in one of the hospital departments. It was Javier, in pale green scrubs. He was working, talking to another person who must have been cropped out of the picture.

But it was the Spanish words that really captured her attention. They were asking questions about why the Conde of Maravilla was at St Aelina's when he had his own post in Madrid. There was also another connecting story and a whole host of speculation.

Caitlin's mouth was instantly dry. There was another photo, of a woman with blonde hair, coiled perfectly, and dressed in a green designer dress. Elisabeth—the German Duchess, his long-standing fiancée, who was apparently broken-hearted over Javier's actions. Her heart stopped. How many years did the paper claim he'd been engaged? Twelve. Twelve?

No. That couldn't be right. She flicked again, this time finding a search engine and putting in Javier and Elisabeth's names. Dozens of pictures appeared. In all of them they were side by side and looking entirely the part as two members of the aristocracy.

It still irked that Elisabeth was a Duchess, even though it was irrelevant. Javier had spoken about Elisabeth in the past tense. But this article didn't. It maintained that Javier and Elisabeth were still together. Her blood ran cold.

Had she just slept with some other woman's fiancé? It referred to a very long engagement. Had he also been engaged to Elisabeth the last time they'd slept together? Had he even been engaged to her when they were graduating from medical school?

Fury started somewhere around her toes

and quickly bubbled up through her chest. This just couldn't be happening.

She strode back through to the bedroom, where Javier was standing with his scrub trousers on, rubbing his damp hair with a towel.

'What is this?' she asked, thrusting the phone towards him.

He was clearly stunned. 'What?' His brow creased in confusion and he reached out to take her phone.

She watched his eyes scanning the screen, his head shaking slowly. 'No,' he murmured. 'No, this isn't true.'

His eyes met hers. 'Tell me you don't believe a word of this.'

'What words?' she snapped. 'That you're still engaged? That she's broken-hearted. That you've been with her for years. Which words am I not to believe?'

He looked stung. 'Elisabeth and I are not together. And she's not broken-hearted,' he insisted. 'She's married to someone else now. And she's very happy—and I'm very happy for her.'

'How on earth can I believe that when the papers are printing things like this? They even have a photo of you somewhere in St

Aelina's. What about the staff there—what about the patients and their privacy? All because the press want to follow you. And how long were you actually engaged for, Javier? Twelve years? That's what they say. Were you engaged the first time we slept together, or were you only engaged this time around?'

She couldn't think straight. The fury was consuming her.

'Stop it,' he snapped. 'I wasn't engaged to Elisabeth either time we slept together. I told you about her. I told you things didn't work out between us—even though I tried. She never loved me, and I never loved her. That's why we're not together any more. She's no more broken-hearted than I was. This is all nonsense!'

'How can I trust a single word you say, when the papers print these kinds of things about you?'

Javier was stunned. He wasn't even sure how to start this conversation. It all seemed so ridiculous to him. Of course Elisabeth's marriage had been a secret. The press had never got hold of that story, and he'd kept his promise to Elisabeth to allow her to have some privacy in her new life. But he could understand why Caitlin would find this hard to believe.

He hadn't known Elisabeth very well twelve years ago. Their parents had been friends, in the way that titled people from fellow countries are. The press seemed to have conveniently forgotten that.

But, more importantly, didn't Caitlin appreciate how much she meant to him? Surely he'd spent the last few weeks showing her how much this time had meant to him. How he wished they could have a different future.

Had he imagined their connection? Why on earth would Caitlin believe something printed in some local rag rather than what he told her?

Javier held up his hands and took a long, deep breath. 'Trust? You want to talk about trust? Yes, let's do that, Caitlin.'

'What's that supposed to mean?'

'You've never really confided in me. You've never really trusted me. Do you trust anyone?'

He watched as Caitlin visibly drew back. He knew he should stop. But he couldn't stop himself. This all seemed such a mess. He hated the press. Hated that he'd had to put on a face for them. To live up to his parents' expectations. Now, they were interfering with the final day he would have with Caitlin. He had one more surgery to do, and then he could leave. But he'd wanted them to part under the best circumstances.

'What kind of thing is that to say?' she snapped.

He should stop. But he couldn't. He was too impassioned about this. It was as if all his frustrations were bubbling up inside him. Maybe it was because he knew they couldn't be together. There wasn't a way to work this out. They both knew that.

Had they been hoping for an unrealistic future—hoping they could spend one last night together and walk away with no regrets? Maybe this was always going to happen.

'It's the truth,' he said with a sigh. 'I get it. You never really told me how tough things were for you growing up. I was right there, Caitlin. I wanted to help; I wanted to listen. I understand you find it tough trusting people. But you should trust me; I'm telling you the truth.'

She shook her head. 'How can I trust you? Did it slip your mind that Elisabeth had got married? No one else seems to know about it.'

'What does that have to do with anything?'

'It's just one of the truths you didn't share with me.'

He was getting nowhere. She was slipping away from him. And maybe this was for the best. Maybe they were meant to leave things like this. Maybe arguing made it easier to walk away.

He took a breath. 'You don't trust me. You know me, Caitlin. You know me better than anyone else, and yet you still can't believe what I tell you. If you don't trust me, what do we even have?' His thoughts were turning in circles. It was probably best that this was over. It would do no good for him to go back home and start fretting about Caitlin. It would be hard enough to walk away from his career and the job he loved. The truth was he was probably better off alone. He already knew he wouldn't get over Caitlin and at least this way he could walk away and try his best to concentrate on his new life.

'Caitlin, stop. There's no point fighting here. We know this can't work.' He put his hand on his heart. 'I want to be with you. I'm not interested in anyone else. But we both know I have to change my life, and there isn't a way to make this work. I want us to be friends. I wish we could spend the rest of our lives the way we have spent the last two weeks.' He shook his head. 'But I just don't know how to make this work. And if you don't trust me, why should we even try?'

Caitlin's face was a picture of fury. It was so unlike her. 'How can I trust you when you can't tell me the truth? You deliberately kept the secrets about Elisabeth's marrying someone else from the whole world. Why didn't you announce your engagement was over? Did you want people to think you were cheating on her with me? How shallow does that make me look? Did you think about how that might ruin my reputation? Or did that never even figure in your thoughts? Did I just not figure in your thoughts? Because, let's face it, I'm never going to fit into your world. Elisabeth would. She's a duchess. But me? Is that why you let everyone think you were still engaged? Was it easier that way? Are you embarrassed by me? Don't you think I'm good enough for you? Is that what all this is really about? You probably have another member of the aristocracy out there, ready to fill the place as your new Countess. Someone who will give up their own life and hopes and dreams, just park it all, to go and spend their time at your side, looking after the estate. That's what you want, isn't it?'

He didn't recognise the woman in front of

him. It was clear that, right now, it didn't matter what Javier said, Caitlin wouldn't be listening. He wanted to deny all that she'd just accused him of. He hated that she even had those thoughts. But everything just seemed too far gone.

Before he had a chance to say another word she turned on her heel and headed to the door. 'Enough,' she called over her shoulder. 'I'm going to check on your sister. Once I'm happy, she can go home. I'll send you any instructions by email. We don't need to talk again. Let's face it, we managed twelve years without talking, I'm sure we can manage another twelve!'

There were angry tears spilling down her face. He wanted to reach out and grab her. Tell her to take a breath, to think about this, to give them some time, to give them a chance to try and come out of all this as friends.

But Javier wouldn't do that. It would only inflame the situation and make things worse. And that was the last thing he needed to do right now.

He watched her walk away with a sick feeling in his stomach. He put his hands on the desk in his room and took a few breaths. He wished he didn't need to go back into the hospital but he had one last surgery.

He steadied his breathing. After a few moments, he reached for his scrub top and pulled it over his head. He winced as he caught the aroma of Caitlin's perfume. It brought with it a whole host of memories he couldn't possibly deal with.

He stared at the bed. It too would likely smell of her skin, her shampoo, her perfume. There was no way he could sleep in those sheets tonight.

He picked up his room key and walked quickly out of the room. One more surgery, a check on his sister and then he would be gone.

He could make arrangements for his sister's care to be transferred closer to home. That way he wouldn't have to deal with Caitlin again.

And, painful as it was, he would have to get on with his life.

CHAPTER TEN

CAITLIN COULDN'T THINK STRAIGHT. She just knew she had to get away from Javier. Being in his presence hurt. He'd told her in part about Elisabeth, but not all about her. Not the parts that seemed important to Caitlin.

Tears flooded down her face as she strode through the hospital corridors, ignoring elevators and taking the steps to the fourth floor two at a time. She was hardly even breathless when she reached her own department. Being a runner meant that it took a lot to get her out of breath.

One of her nursing staff caught the expression on her face and put out her hand gently to halt her stride down the corridor. 'Caitlin,' she said quietly, 'what's wrong?'

She couldn't answer that question. She just shook her head.

She continued towards Natalia's room. No

one had paged her so she had to assume that everything was fine.

When she arrived, Natalia was sitting up in bed, her colour good and the readings on her monitor exactly where Caitlin would want them to be.

It didn't matter how angry she was with Javier. Her patients were always her priority.

'How do you feel?'

Natalia raised her hand to her chest wall. 'Apart from the fact you prised me open, surprisingly good.' She shifted her shoulders. 'I'm sore, obviously. But sore in a different way from before. The tightness in my chest has changed. The kind of underlying heaviness isn't there now.'

Caitlin nodded, understanding. 'I'm glad—all your signs are good. From my perspective the procedure went very well. All being well, I expect you to make an excellent recovery.'

Natalia gave a huge sigh of relief. 'You don't know how happy that makes me. I was so worried before the surgery—you know, just silly stuff. But I know Javier was worried too. It's such a relief to have it all over with. I can't wait to get back to work.'

Caitlin froze. She wasn't quite sure what to say. 'Are you going back to the vineyard?'

'Of course.' Natalia's brow furrowed. 'Why would you ask that?'

Caitlin took a deep breath. 'Because I understood that Javier was going back to take over.'

Natalia's frown deepened. Then a look of exasperation filled her face. 'This is my mother, isn't it? She and Javier think I'm some fragile girl who needs protecting. But the estate is my job, my dream. Javier doesn't know a single thing about running the estate, or about looking after a vineyard. He would be absolutely crazy to give up his job.' She paused and then looked at Caitlin again. 'And to give up you.'

She must have read the shocked expression on Caitlin's face because she continued. 'I might just have had heart surgery, but I couldn't help but notice everything else that's been going on around me. I've never seen Javier so happy. I always wondered how long it would take you two to finally get together, and now it's happened it has to continue. Don't think I've missed a single thing.'

Caitlin couldn't quite find the words. She shook her head. 'Javier and I can't have a relationship. He has to go back and be the Count. He says it's his duty.'

Natalia threw up her hands. 'He can be the Count and still be a surgeon. He trained for years to do this job. He can't walk away.' She started to look annoyed. 'I'm perfectly capable of managing the estate, and I can do it much better than he ever could. Where is the sense in all this?'

Caitlin was very still. 'Has Javier not spoken to you about all this?'

Natalia shook her head. 'He'll be protecting me, of course. Sometimes I think my brother just doesn't get it. Surgery is his dream and the estate is mine. I'm not going to give up my dream for him. I just need a few weeks for a full recovery, then I'll be better than before.'

Caitlin could feel a whole host of sensations sweeping over her. 'Have you told Javier this is how you feel about everything?'

Natalia gave Caitlin a sorry smile. 'Javier needs to learn to stop feeling guilty over our father's death. He seems to blame himself— he thinks that he should have predicted it. But he's not a mind-reader or a miracle-worker; he's a person. He's a surgeon—and a very good one—but he can't prevent every death. He thinks that he disappointed our father by not marrying Elisabeth. But you can't marry someone you don't love—' she looked Caitlin in the eye '—can you?'

Caitlin's skin chilled. 'Javier has made headlines this morning,' she said numbly.

'Really?' Natalia reached for her phone and swiped it open; within a minute she was shaking her head scornfully. 'Well, the only thing that's truthful in this is that he's here at St Aelina's. Everything else is ridiculous.'

'All of it?'

'Of course.' The furrow in Natalia's brow returned. 'Don't tell me you believed any of this?'

But she had. She'd been consumed with rage and had only thought about herself. She'd had no idea that Javier had carried guilt over his father's death. Guilt that had likely played into his decision to go back home and take over.

Natalia spoke quietly. 'Elisabeth got married in secret a few months ago. Her husband has some health issues. She didn't want the press following them everywhere and snooping into every part of their lives. She wanted some privacy, some time to themselves.' Natalia swept a strand of hair from her face. 'I know that she planned to reveal her marriage in a few months' time.' She shook her head.

'This is just bad timing. Her husband is also having surgery this week. He, like me, will hopefully make a full recovery. Then they can release a statement and a photo of their wedding.'

Caitlin's mouth was horribly dry. If Natalia knew all this, then Javier did too. If only she'd asked more questions. If only she'd dug deeper, she might have discovered all this and had the chance to talk to him about it.

Elisabeth's husband was having surgery; of course Javier would have the good grace to stay silent, in order to allow them the privacy they wished for. It was just the kind of person he was—and Caitlin knew that.

He'd told her earlier that she hadn't opened up to him; now she was seeing that he hadn't opened up to her either and she wished she'd worked harder to persuade him.

Pieces were falling into place in her head. She'd been so angry, so worked up, she hadn't really given him a chance to talk.

She glanced at the clock on the wall. Javier had one more surgery. That was where he would be. She had to talk to him.

She was back down the stairs in a flash, not caring who watched her running down the corridor. By the time she reached Theatre she already knew what was happening by the vibe of the people around her. It was professionally quiet. Surgery had started.

She found the theatre manager. 'What time did they go in?' she asked.

The theatre manager looked up from her desk. 'Who?'

'Javier Torres. Theatre Seven.'

The theatre manager turned to her board. 'Four p.m.'

Caitlin's brain raced. The surgery Javier was performing usually took a few hours. It was likely he would not be out until after six p.m.

Just at that moment her pager sounded. She looked down and flinched at the message.

High risk alert. All personnel to Theatre.

The theatre manager's page went off at the same time and she picked up her phone. The conversation she had with the ER took seconds. She slammed the phone down and ran around the desk. Staff were already emerging in response to the page. 'Theatre Four, everyone,' the manager shouted. 'Pregnant woman being resuscitated. They suspect a massive MI.'

There was no shouting, no panic. People moved seamlessly and without any other instruction. Caitlin was in Theatre Four in an instant. She would need to do an emergency angio. The clot blocking this woman's artery had to be removed. Caitlin knew she wouldn't be the first to assist. An obstetric surgeon ran into the theatre beside her, quickly followed by a neonatal nurse pushing a warming crib. Caitlin moved to the sinks, the surgeon right behind her, and both started scrubbing.

The doors burst open behind them. The ER doctor was on the top of the trolley performing cardiac massage. Another member of staff was standing on the runners, bagging the woman to try and keep the flow of oxygen around her body.

The anaesthetist appeared, took one look at the scene and moved into place. 'Report!' he shouted.

Caitlin and the obstetrician turned to don gowns and masks.

Caitlin helped assist in the move from the emergency trolley to the operating table. Once she'd helped pulled the woman over, she connected some electrodes to ensure they could pick up any heart activity and reconnected the electronic BP cuff.

It was all hands on deck. She was prepared to assist in any way in a situation like this. If she had to do the angio while cardiac massage was ongoing, she knew this poor woman's chances would be slim.

The obstetrician listened to the report from the ER doctor as he jumped down from the trolley and one of the theatre technicians took his place, continuing massage.

He exchanged a glance with the anaesthetist. 'We're going to get this baby out. Mum has been down seven minutes already.'

The anaesthetist agreed. The obstetrician turned to Caitlin. 'As soon as I've got the baby out you can start, as I stitch her up.'

'Do you need assistance?' asked the ER doc.

Caitlin looked around. Javier was busy. She had no idea where her other staff were. 'I do,' she said quickly.

'Time,' shouted the nurse in charge.

Everything in Theatre was precise, and this team moved in perfect synchronicity.

'Stop massage!' shouted the obstetrician and they all watched the monitor for a second to see if there would be any heart activity.

There was one blip, and then silence.

'Continue,' instructed the obstetrician and moved into position.

Santiago burst through the doors just as the obstetrician made the first cut. The baby was out in under a minute and into his waiting hands.

Caitlin couldn't bear to watch her friend, and wondered where he'd just come running from. She held her breath, waiting for any sound from the baby.

But Caitlin had a job to do. She'd come here to speak to Javier, full of regrets and wanting a chance to talk. But maybe this was fate.

Who knew where she might have been in the hospital when this page had sounded? She might even have been outside the hospital. Officially, she wasn't on call; her page had sounded because Javier was already in surgery.

She didn't have time to think about anything else. A woman's life was at stake. She moved to put on her gloves before she started her procedure.

The ER doctor was in position next to her, as her screens flickered on. She made a small incision at the groin as the obstetrician started stitching the womb. It would be difficult to see the blockage while the heart, chest and vessels would be moving. But this had to be done. It didn't matter how hard it was.

'Any history?' she asked the ER doc as she prepared to thread the catheter into place.

'Presented with chest pain. Thirty-four years old, para three, gestation thirty-seven weeks. Blood pressure crashed, short episode of ventricular tachycardia before she arrested.'

There was a cry from the newly delivered baby, followed by an audible gasp of relief from many of the staff in the room. Caitlin could feel her own heart thudding in her chest. The baby cried again, more of a whimper this time. But it was alive. She didn't even know if it was a boy or girl yet. But she had to keep her head in the game.

'Medical history?'

'Didn't get it, I'm afraid. We don't have medical notes for her at this hospital. Our medical records team are contacting other maternity units as an emergency.'

Caitlin nodded. She raised her voice. 'I'm going to have to ask massage to stop in a few seconds.' The red-faced technician in position nodded.

A colleague spoke up. 'I'll take over.'

No one could keep up cardiac massage for long. It was best the role was rotated among other staff. Caitlin couldn't help but wish that Javier was in Theatre with her. He might have some other ideas.

'I need someone to time for me,' Caitlin continued.

'Done,' shouted the theatre manager.

She used her best judgement as to when the catheter would be in the optimum position. She nodded to the ER doc, who had clearly worked on angios before. He moved into position, ready to inject the dye.

Caitlin timed everything in her head. 'And... stop. Time.'

The massage stopped. 'Now,' she said to the ER doc, who injected the dye.

She watched the screen to see the blockage. It was huge. Her hands moved like lightning, threading up the balloon and inflating it to try and relieve the blockage. She was praying she would do everything correctly. She'd never wanted Javier beside her so badly in her entire life. She couldn't let them see how terrified she was.

'Thirty seconds,' came the call.

She held her breath. It seemed as if the blood was thinking about moving again. She really needed to insert a stent. But unblocking the vessel was the biggest priority. Depending on what happened next, she might have to insert a stent later.

There was a quiver...something. All eyes went to the monitor. A few beeps. Caitlin was praying these weren't just ectopic, irregular beats.

Then something else happened. It seemed like an age, but then there were more regular beats.

The obstetrician looked up from his stitching. 'We need to talk anticoagulant,' he said.

Caitlin nodded. This patient would routinely require some kind of anticoagulant to stop formation of another blood clot. But right now, after an emergency section, it was essential that the uterus contracted properly, and this woman would have surgical wounds too. The balance would be tricky.

'I'm going to stop here,' Caitlin announced. 'The blockage is cleared and I can time her stent around other treatment.'

She couldn't help but wonder about some kind of unknown clotting disorder. It seemed far too risky to proceed without more medical details. Right now, St Aelina's had a baby and mother who'd survived a situation that could easily have gone wrong. She wanted time to assess further.

As she withdrew the catheter and applied pressure to the incision site, the theatre manager put a hand on her shoulder. 'Let me just say, Caitlin, I've never been so pleased to see you.'

Caitlin gave a nervous laugh and shook her head. 'I actually can't believe it.'

She looked around the room. All of the staff had performed magnificently, but a few of them looked quite stunned.

'We'll need to do a debrief,' she said in a lower voice.

'Agreed,' said the theatre manager, clearly assessing the room the same way she had.

The anaesthetist moved into position, giving instructions and taking over. Caitlin was relieved. Santiago gave her a nod as he wheeled the crib out, obviously taking the new delivery to NICU.

Caitlin's eyes went to the clock on the wall in Theatre. It was after seven.

Her heart flipped. Javier. She had to get to Javier.

But she had to wait. She couldn't just turn and walk out. She moved over to the anaesthetist. 'Do you still need me?'

He looked at her and gave a brief nod. 'Not right now. But come to Recovery in an hour. I'm going to recheck her bloods and we can confer with the obstetrician over further treatment.'

An hour. She had an hour. She could make that work.

She pulled off her surgical gown and mask and stuffed them into the nearest waste bin.

She walked, telling herself not to run, as she exited the door and headed to Theatre Seven. But it was dark—it had been shut down.

Her heart started to beat faster. She moved quickly to the changing rooms. Empty. There were a few other people, who glanced at her then put their heads down and continued changing.

She moved again, through the theatre complex, along other hospital corridors and heading to the exit. Should she go back to her own floor—might he be with Natalia?

Something told her no.

She was now half running, half walking to the exit. His hotel was straight across the road. The traffic was busy—of course it was. She dodged through the cars and buses and made it to the entrance.

Thankfully, the doorman must have recognised her because he didn't stop the slightly red-faced woman in scrubs.

She moved over to the reception desk. She'd never spoken to the staff here before—she'd never had to. Javier had always taken her straight up to his room.

The woman behind the desk gave her a curious stare. 'I'm here to see Javier Torres,' she said, knowing there was a catch in her voice. The emotion was telling on her now. She'd had a terrible argument with the man she loved, then performed one of her most stressful surgeries. All she needed right now was to see Javier, to have a chance to speak to him.

Even now she was aware that she'd need to go back to Recovery soon to discuss the patient she'd barely had a chance to meet.

The woman behind the desk hadn't moved. She wore an immaculate suit and her hair was swept back in a neat bun. Her red lips were pristine. 'I'm sorry,' she said politely, 'but Señor Torres, the Conde de Maravilla, has already checked out. I believe his flight is leaving shortly.'

Caitlin's heart sank. Barcelona was a sprawling city; the airport was far from here.

It would take nearly an hour to get there, and there was no way she would reach him in time. She didn't even need to guess that he wouldn't be flying commercial. It would be a private flight.

He was gone. She'd been too late. She'd missed the chance to speak to him, to tell him how she felt, and how sorry she was about everything.

Her legs started to sag as the day's events caught up with her.

'Miss, are you all right?'

The woman clicked her fingers and the doorman appeared behind her and helped her into a chair. Before she had a chance to say a word, a bottle of cold water was pressed into her hand.

She breathed. Once. Twice. Then pressed the water to her forehead.

'Can I get you anything else?' The woman from the reception desk was kneeling in front her. She had remarkably kind eyes.

Caitlin shook her head. 'No, thank you. It's my own fault. I've just missed the chance to make up with a friend.'

The woman gave her a sympathetic glance. 'Maybe you'll get another chance.'

Caitlin knew she was trying to be kind, and

she pushed herself to her feet. 'By then I'll be too late,' she said as she headed to the door, keeping the bottle in her hand. 'My chance will be gone.' She looked down at her feet, knowing she only had herself to blame.

Two chances with Javier. Both of them had been ruined. There was no chance to go back in time in this life. She'd heard enough sad stories as a doctor to know this was true. It was time to get back to the only thing she could actually get right.

Being a surgeon.

CHAPTER ELEVEN

JAVIER WAS HEARTBROKEN. There was no other description of how he felt. The look in Caitlin's eyes when she'd been angry with him would stay in his head for a long time.

They'd both agreed to a short-term thing. Maybe it would be better if he wiped the final twenty-four hours from his head and just kept the rest of the memories.

He'd arrived back at the estate after stopping off at the hospital in Madrid and officially handing in his notice. The board of the hospital were shocked. They'd hoped to keep Javier Torres for the next twenty years—and he would gladly have stayed there.

There had been many offers made. Reduced hours, some remote working. More staff. But for Javier this seemed like the time to rip the sticking plaster off straight away, rather than edge it off slowly.

He couldn't do half a job at his hospital in Madrid and half a job on the family estate. That way mistakes would happen. And that wasn't how Javier functioned. No matter what he was doing, he wanted to be at the top of his game, whether that was being a cardio-thoracic surgeon or the Conde de Maravilla.

So he'd arranged to work his notice over the next few months, hand over his patients and take some of his outstanding leave.

That meant he was now back at the family estate, wondering where on earth to start.

As he stood on the balcony, looking over the vineyards, his mother came to join him. She gave him an enthusiastic hug. 'I am so pleased about Natalia. I was so frightened for her surgery.'

Although he'd never felt this low before, he returned his mother's hug with genuine relief. 'I was worried too, even though I trusted her surgeon. I know that I've had a million similar conversations with patients' relatives before, but it's different when the patient is family.'

His mother leaned back, her arms still around him, and gave an understanding nod. She reached out and touched his cheek. 'What's wrong, Javier? You should be happy.

Your sister will be well again. But all I see is sadness in your face. I don't see you often enough. Has something happened?'

He didn't really know where to start. He turned away and put his hands on the carved stone wall that made up the ornate balcony overlooking the estate. As he looked, he breathed deeply.

'It's just a lot to take in,' he said softly. 'I love this place, but I've never taken an interest in the business side of the estate before. And now I feel as if I've already let Papá down. I should have paid attention earlier. There will be so much to learn, and the vineyard has always done so well. People love the organic produce from Maravilla. I'm worried that I won't have the knowledge to continue the business the way it should.'

His mother touched his hand, concern filling her face. 'Why on earth do you think you've let your *papá* down?'

Javier dipped his head. 'Because I didn't want to be here. I didn't want to do this. Papá hoped I would marry Elisabeth but...' he breathed out through his nose '... I just couldn't do it. I didn't love her. Not the way she deserved to be loved. Not the way anyone deserves to be loved.'

He lifted his eyes and looked back out over the vineyards. They stretched for kilometres. He could see people tending them even now. The work here never finished. A truck was taking the road to the side of the driveway, heading down to pick up the organic fruit from one of their orchards.

But Javier had forgotten just how astute his mother was. She squeezed his hand. 'How does someone deserve to be loved?'

His answer came with no hesitation. 'Completely. With no secrets. With compromise, and with trust.' He gave a sad smile. 'As equal partners. Even though you will always put that other person first—no matter what they say.'

His mother was watching him carefully, affection in her eyes. 'First of all, your father loved you with his whole heart.' She put her hand on her chest. 'If he were still here, all he would want is for you and Natalia to be happy.' She shook her head. 'Yes, your father was disappointed when you broke off your engagement. He thought you and Elisabeth were perfect for each other. But only you could know that, Javier—not us.'

'But then he took ill and died, and I never got the chance to talk to him again. I never got the chance to say sorry. I hadn't seen him; I might have been able to pick up what was wrong with him.' His voice broke. 'I might have had a chance to save him. To save Papá—if I hadn't been so proud and foolish.'

'No,' his mother cut in. 'Javier, you could never have saved him. None of us could have saved him. I was here. It was over in seconds. Your father never knew anything about it. He'd had no symptoms. You know what he was like; he used to tell people he was as healthy as an ox. And now—' she looked out over the estate '—I know it was the best way for your father to go. I was shocked at the time. Devastated.' She gave him a warm smile. 'And even though my son is a very special surgeon, I had no idea what an arteriovenous malformation was. I can still barely say it.' She waved her hand towards the lush gardens of the estate. The lawn was manicured, the paths carefully paved. A large three-tier water fountain was just beneath them in a circular bed. Across the lawn, there were various shaped topiary, accompanied by splashes of colour in further circular beds. 'Look at this. Can you imagine how your father would have been if he'd had something like a stroke and couldn't get out in his gardens or vineyards again? He would have been miserable, and unbearable.'

She took a deep breath. 'I lost the love of my life, Javier. But I didn't have the pain of watching him suffer.'

Javier was looking at the lawns too. Deep down he did love this place. He always had. It was home. It was family. And could he see himself growing old here? Yes, he probably could.

'I'll do this, Mamá; I'll make this work. I'll make sure the business is every bit as successful as when Papá ran it.' He was determined. He couldn't let his family down.

His mother's voice had laughter in it as she put her hand on his arm again. 'Javier, you need to listen. You need to stop shutting the world out and being so single-minded when you feel pushed into a corner.'

She gave him an amused glance. 'Let's go for a walk.'

He was surprised. 'A walk?'

'Yes, I want to show you some things.'

Javier nodded and joined his mother as she led him outside; they walked down the intricately paved paths towards the long driveway, and then down one of the roads which led from it. He knew exactly where this went.

They walked for around half a mile. It was a beautiful day. The sun was high in the sky, and the air was warm and dry.

As they neared the vineyards and orchards, many of the staff waved or gave him a nod. They were all hard at work. A few came up to ask after Natalia. Javier and his mother answered all their questions. The vintner, the sales manager and viticulturist were all busy.

They carried on past the entrance to the vineyards and on to the orchards. Javier's mother held out her hand. 'The shift to organic working was already in hand before your father died. Natalia has handled every part of it since. We didn't have too much work to do from the processes already in place, but the technicalities were crucial. Natalia was key to this.'

She turned to Javier with a wide smile on her face. 'This is your sister's dream, and she is flourishing. She is maintaining the traditions, whilst bringing in new ideas. It's the perfect combination.'

'But the stress it puts her under...'

'Should be managed by her physician. From what I understand, Natalia's operation was a success. I spoke to her surgeon this morning.' There was a gleam in his mother's eye.

'You did?'

'She phoned me, with Natalia's permission. She gave me the full rundown on the surgery, and how long the recovery process should take. She was confident that Natalia should be back to full health in a matter of weeks.'

Javier didn't speak, just started to compute things in his head. He gave a slow nod. 'And if she needs assistance in the future?'

'Then, as a family, we will discuss what works best. I've already employed two very capable assistants for the vineyards and orchards.'

His mother looked out across the orchards with pride. She wasn't looking at Javier right now. 'Do you want to tell me about her?'

He swallowed. His mother had always read him better than anyone. 'Tell you about who?'

'The person who made you realise what love is?'

His shoulders sagged. 'You've met her.'

'The brilliant, feisty Scottish fellow medical student who visited a few times in the holidays? The girl who was never scared to ask questions?' Her smile grew as she kept looking at the orchards. 'The girl who turned into a very capable surgeon who has just saved the life of my daughter?'

Javier nodded. 'You knew?'

'Your sister may have dropped a few hints.'

Javier held out his hands. 'But she doesn't want this, Mamá. How on earth can we have any kind of relationship?'

'But you don't want this either,' his mother said plainly.

Javier looked at his past, his present and his future lying in front of him. It stretched for miles. Happy memories, a wonderful childhood, good people who worked hard.

'At least not like this,' she added. 'Not as a business.'

Javier let the tension release from his shoulders. 'You're right,' he admitted. 'But I feel if I say that I am letting you down.'

His mother's voice was kind. 'The only way you let me down is if you don't follow your heart. I lost the love of my life. Don't lose yours. Don't try and fulfil a family obligation that makes you miserable and lose the joy from your life. You have a wonderful set of skills, Javier. I am so proud that my son can save lives on a daily basis. So was your father. We remain immensely proud of you. I want you to be happy. That is the most important thing for me, that *both* my children are happy.'

The relief flooding through his body was like a welcome balm, the words from his mother exactly what he wanted to hear.

'So, it's decided,' she continued. 'Once Natalia gets the all-clear she will officially take over again here. You will be free to pursue your wonderful work, and to marry the woman that you love.'

The expression on his mother's face was triumphant, and Javier couldn't bear to reveal the part that made his heart heavy. That for him and Caitlin it was probably already too late.

Caitlin was sitting in St Aelina's park. She'd already run around the perimeter twice this morning. Usually running helped deal with any frustrations. But not today. The frustrations were etched into her very soul.

Javier had been right about so many things. She'd let her past impact upon her future. It didn't matter that she had friends here. It didn't matter that she had a job she loved. She'd never felt so empty, or alone.

She leaned back against the park bench and

lifted her face to the early morning sun. At some point, this had to feel better.

She'd spent the last few days doing her job automatically. Thankfully, both mum and baby were doing well. The little girl, Rosa, was breathing and feeding well. After being ventilated for a day, mum had her sedation decreased and was breathing on her own and conscious, between bouts of sleeping. She was still very tired and would require further investigations. But she knew her baby was here and was safe. That was the most important thing.

Caitlin should be relieved and proud of what she'd achieved with a few minutes' notice. As a mentor, she would normally have taken copious notes to use the case as a teaching episode for future students. And she likely would. But right now she just couldn't face it.

She was thinking about other things. Like Javier, and the expression on his face when she'd told him she couldn't trust him. The word *wounded* wouldn't come close to how he'd looked, and her gut told her she'd ruined their friendship for ever.

She was telling herself it was for the best. She didn't want to be friends with Javier. She wanted much, much more than that. But it couldn't work between them. And even that thought brought fresh tears to her eyes.

How could it be that you could know who your perfect mate was, but the world conspired against you to stop you from being together? It seemed like some rotten kind of fairy tale.

It didn't help that the newspaper involved had printed a retraction. She didn't doubt that lawyers had been involved somewhere. Or that she suspected a conversation had taken place with Elisabeth. A picture had emerged of a beaming Elisabeth on her wedding day. The accompanying text was clear. The Duchess had married the man of her dreams and was entirely happy. Her husband had recently had a small procedure carried out, and both of them would be available to speak to the press shortly. She had certainly not been brokenhearted over the breakup of her engagement to Javier Torres, but she thought he was a fine surgeon and wished him well for the future.

Caitlin had never felt like such a fool. She wondered if she would end up one of those ancient old spinster ladies who told stories to young people, about her days of yelling at a Spanish Count, wrongly accusing him of being a lying cheat.

They would be right to shake their heads at her and tell her she was a fool.

She sighed and watched as a few mothers with buggies walked past; others were jogging around the perimeter of the park like she had, and someone was sitting under a tree, reading a book with a coffee next to them.

She had work to do. She had patients to see. Natalia would be leaving tomorrow. Her recovery had been excellent. Her last link to Javier would be gone.

But she wasn't tempted to try and delay Natalia's discharge. Caitlin would never do something like that. This was all for the best. Natalia should go home to complete her recovery, get back to normal and resume her life.

She stood up and walked back to the hospital, ready to shower and change in her office. As she strode along the corridor the hospital director came towards her, an electronic tablet in her hand.

'Ah, Ms McKenzie,' she said. 'Quick chat. You still have four weeks leave to take this year.'

Caitlin blinked. Holidays weren't something she thought about much, too busy arranging her next set of surgeries.

'I haven't planned yet when to take them.'

'How about next week?' The director smiled.

'Why next week?'

'Forgive me,' said the director, 'but there needs to be some work done in Theatre Six. It's where you perform most of your surgeries and should only take a few days. I'd like to schedule it as soon as possible, and it would seem fortuitous to have it coincide with your holiday. You've been working very hard; don't think I don't notice. I've got to have my surgeons well rested.'

She said the statement like a question. Caitlin had the distinct impression she was being told to take holiday rather than being asked.

'I suppose I could work that,' she replied. 'There are only a few procedures that would need rescheduling.'

'Perfect.' The director smiled, tapping something into her electronic tablet and walking back down the corridor, clearly off to find her next victim.

Caitlin gave a small smile and walked into her office. A holiday wouldn't be such a disaster. It might give her a change of scene. Just what she needed right now.

As she walked into the office and switched on the shower in the bathroom, she spotted a note on her desk.

She picked it up.

Can Natalia Torres have a quick chat with you?

It had been left by her secretary. Of course she could do that.

She showered and changed and walked back along to the rooms on the fourth floor.

Natalia was sitting by her bedside in yoga pants and a button-down top. She looked relaxed and happy. The only thing that revealed her surgery was the edge of a surgical dressing near the button of her top.

'Hi, Natalia. I heard you wanted to see me. Is everything okay? Are you feeling all right?'

Natalia nodded. 'Great, but I wondered if you could do me a favour, part as a friend and part as my doctor?'

Caitlin was curious. She sat down next to Natalia. 'Of course. What is it?'

Natalia swallowed, fixing her eyes on Caitlin's. 'I wondered if you would accompany me home…and monitor me for a few days.'

'Oh...' The request took Caitlin by surprise; it was the last thing she was expecting.

'Isn't Javier taking you home?'

Natalia shook her head. 'He's had to go back to work in Madrid. He will eventually be back at home and able to monitor me, but he has some responsibilities he has to take care of in Madrid. They'd already been so good to him and gave him a few weeks' leave to be here. And, between you and me, I've always been nervous about flights in the helicopter.'

Caitlin nodded. She understood just how busy cardiothoracic surgeons could be. In a way, by doing extra surgeries at night, he had helped her lower her own waiting list. It was part of the reason she could take a holiday now.

Although the request was unusual, it wasn't out of the question. 'Well...' she smiled '... I've just been given a week's leave myself. So I'm happy to accompany you home and ensure you get settled.' She touched Natalia's hand. She hadn't expected Natalia to be so concerned about her recovery. 'This is all going to go fine, honestly.'

Natalia breathed a sigh of relief and nodded. 'Thank you. I appreciate you doing this

for me. And you'll get to see all the changes
on the estate too. Wait until you see the orchards. It's not just apples and oranges now.
I have lemons, apricots, pears and peaches.'

Her face was glowing. Caitlin could see it
as plain as day; Natalia loved the estate and
the job she did there.

Although her stomach twisted uncomfortably at the thought that all her memories of
the estate were tied up with Javier, she could
do this. She could. It would actually be nice
to see the beautiful ancestral home again, the
well-maintained gardens, and what had been
done with the vineyards and orchards. Javier
wouldn't be there, so she might also have a
chance to see the Condesa again, and offer
her condolences since she'd missed the news
about Javier's father.

Her stomach started to unknot. She was a
grown-up. She could do this. It might even
help her move on and put things behind her.
Maybe, just maybe, she could write a letter
of apology and leave it for Javier somewhere.

Yes, that would be better than an email,
text or phone call. She was more than a little
worried that he wouldn't answer her at the
moment. An old-fashioned handwritten letter
seemed like a better way to deal with things.

She stood up and smiled at Natalia. 'When do you plan to leave? I'll need to pack a few things.'

'First thing in the morning?'

Caitlin nodded. 'Perfect. I'll meet you here first thing.'

Caitlin had remembered about helicopter hair and tied it back in a tight knot to keep it from flapping around her face. This time Natalia didn't require a trolley and monitors for transport. She could walk to the helicopter just like Caitlin, ducking their heads low as they climbed in and fastened their belts. One of Natalia's private staff carried their luggage and this time they had a female pilot.

She gave them a broad smile. 'Just waiting for clearance to take off. Our flight time should be around two hours. Give me a nod if there's anything you want to see on the way.'

They settled in for the flight and took off smoothly. Barcelona passed underneath them in a matter of minutes as they made their way down the Spanish coast.

With her ear defenders in place, the noise of the blades was muffled. Caitlin leaned back to enjoy the ride. She'd only ever flown in a helicopter on a transfer with an emergency patient—and at that time she couldn't look out of a window.

Today she got to enjoy how beautiful Spain was from the air, as they passed over miles and miles of countryside, coastline and some towns.

As they approached the estate, Natalia gave her a nudge to switch her transmitter on and started to point out parts of the estate to her. In the twelve years since she'd seen the place there had been multiple changes visible from the air. New roads, new fields and a few smaller new properties.

Natalia beamed as Caitlin noticed them. 'They are for the staff. We don't just have seasonal staff any more. We have full-time staff, so we needed somewhere for them to stay. We also have a large residence with single rooms for harvest time.'

'It looks magnificent,' Caitlin said with a sigh. She was remembering why she'd loved visiting this place so much. Yes, it was a huge ancestral estate that was somewhere she could never live in or buy in a lifetime, but it was also a family home. It didn't matter that it had forty bedrooms, sprawled throughout the various wings of the estate, it still had a feeling of home. Javier, Natalia and their parents might have had staff, but they'd also made food in their own kitchen, served themselves and curled up on a comfortable sofa at night to watch movies together. It had been in Javier's home that Caitlin had got her first true sense of what family was. They'd all clearly loved each other and cared about each other. She'd witnessed their good-natured teasing. Yes, they were of a different class than she was. But she'd never been made to feel different, or less in any way. They had always been welcoming to her.

The helicopter set down gently on a landing area marked away from the main house. Caitlin and Natalia jumped out as a few staff members from the estate came to greet them.

As Caitlin glanced up at the house she'd once found a little imposing, she was struck by how pleased she was to be here. Even from here, she could pick out the room she'd once stayed in, and her eyes ran along the windows, knowing exactly which room had been Javier's too. She smiled. That was where she would leave her letter, and hope they could at least part as friends.

* * *

Javier crossed the grounds. The helicopter had landed a few minutes before he'd expected it to. He'd offered to collect Natalia in Barcelona, but for some reason she'd asked if someone else could collect her. He could only imagine that Natalia hadn't wanted him to run into Caitlin again. And he was trying not to think about that. Could it be that Caitlin had told her she didn't want to see him again? He'd hoped the retraction in the newspaper might have caught her eye, but there was every chance that she hadn't seen it.

There were a few people standing outside the helicopter. Natalia walked towards him, with two of their staff carrying her luggage, giving him a cheeky wink and smile as she kissed him on the cheek. She didn't say a word, just kept walking towards the house, leaving one person behind.

Caitlin.

Her auburn hair was pulled back from her face. She was wearing a navy jacket and jeans and a white T-shirt. She'd never looked more beautiful.

For a moment all he could do was stare— just like when they'd been on the roof at St Aelina's. His heart was in his mouth.

Caitlin looked as shocked as he was. He realised that Natalia had tricked them both and planned this. He would thank his sister later.

But Javier knew he had to follow every instinct in his body. He ran towards Caitlin, just like she ran towards him. He'd never been so grateful for a hug in his entire life.

'I'm sorry,' she said breathlessly. 'I'm so sorry for everything I said. I didn't mean it. I came to find you, but you'd already left the hotel and I didn't know what to do.' It seemed as if she was going to continue talking, so Javier silenced her with a kiss.

Caitlin responded just the way he'd hoped. His hand went to the back of her head, quickly releasing the tight bun she had at the nape of her neck and letting her auburn hair escape to frame her face.

'I should never have let you go,' he whispered into her ear. 'You're all that I've ever wanted.'

'We can make this work, somehow,' she said, her green eyes sincere. 'I love you, Javier. The most important thing to me is that you're happy. We can stay here this week and find a way to make this work for us both.'

'You love me?' he asked, his hands cupping her cheeks.

She grinned at him. 'I've always loved you. I've just never been brave enough to tell you. And yes, I trust you. I just hated that I thought I might not be good enough for you—might not be enough for you at all.'

He shook his head as he continued to cradle her face. 'How could I give my heart to another when you already had it? You'll always be good enough for me, Caitlin.'

She couldn't stop smiling at him. His eyes were lost in hers. This was where he was supposed to be. Home would be wherever this woman was. And it seemed as if every part of his life was finally beginning to fit.

He gave her another smile. 'You are a magnificent surgeon. I'm reliably informed that Natalia should make a full recovery, and my mother has hired some extra staff to help her.'

'You've spoken to your mother?'

He nodded and pressed his forehead against hers. 'Yes, I've spoken to my mother. She doesn't want me here. She wants me to be a surgeon. She wants me to live the life I should be living with the person I want to live it with.'

'And that's me?'

He hated it that she still needed that reassurance. 'It has always been and will always be you.'

He could feel Caitlin shake a little in his arms. 'Hey,' he said, running his hands through her hair. 'You are the person who makes me feel like home. Not this place. Not anywhere. I will go wherever you go.'

Caitlin's eyes widened. 'But how can we?'

He held his arms wide. 'Say the word; my family know that I want to be with you. They will love you just as much as I do. We can go anywhere, live anywhere, work anywhere. You choose, Caitlin. I'm all yours.'

'Really?' She blinked back the tears that had formed in her eyes. She wrapped her arms around his neck. 'But Javier, I love your house, I love your family. We can find a way to make this work together. Most of all I love you. If I have you, I have everything.'

He pulled her close again. 'Okay, so how about we recreate our past?'

'Which part?' she asked, her nose wrinkled. It was the cutest she'd ever looked.

He whispered in her ear, 'The night we never forgot.' As he pulled back his eyebrows were raised.

Caitlin grinned at him. 'In that case, I think

we have a number of rooms we can choose. Let's try them all.'

So he slipped his hand into hers and led her back towards the house, and recreated that night again and again and again.

EPILOGUE

One year later

'HEY, YOU,' JAVIER SAID, sliding his arms around his wife's waist.

'Hey, you.' She leaned back into him, enjoying the heat from his body. The roof of St Aelina's might be one of their favourite places to escape for private moments, but at times it could be chilly. Barcelona was spread out beneath them, yellow and white lights illuminating various structures within the city. They'd missed the sunset and were left with an inky black sky.

'Did you have a stressful afternoon?' he asked.

She shook her head. 'No, it was fine. Both procedures went well, and I've assessed all my patients for Theatre tomorrow.' She turned her face sideways to catch sight of her husband. 'How about you?'

'Helped Santiago with a cardiac case and saw fifteen patients at a clinic. At least four of them need surgery.'

She reached a hand up to her shoulder and he instantly put his there to join hers. 'Any we can do together?' she asked with a smile. It was her favourite part of her role these days, the surgeries she could do with her husband.

They'd reached a compromise—one which suited them both. They worked two days a week in Madrid and two days a week at St Aelina's in Barcelona, in a unique job-sharing role. It meant that both hospitals had eight sessions with cardiothoracic surgeons, with the only unusual part that they worked the same days together at each hospital.

The conscious decision to have one additional extra day off a week meant that they could choose to visit the family home, Maravilla, or they could choose to spend the day in bed.

'There are always surgeries we can do together,' Javier murmured in her ear, nuzzling her neck. 'I'm starting to like this,' he joked. 'Easier access to your neck.'

Caitlin had decided to cut her long hair to a more manageable length the day before.

She was still getting used to the length, just hitting her shoulders, and had blinked a few times today as she'd passed a reflective surface and wondered who she was looking at.

'Just trying to save some time,' she said breezily. 'Who wants to spend so long drying their hair when we can find other things to do?'

He kissed the skin at the base of her neck and she started to giggle. 'Stop it, you'll put me off the gorgeous view of our city, and my memories of that night a year ago.'

Javier lifted his head. 'You thought I'd forget, didn't you?'

'Never,' she said, laughing.

'How could I forget the first night I saw you again after twelve years? Talk about making a guy wait.'

She turned in his arms so she was facing him instead of staring at the city. 'Some people might consider me worth the wait.'

'Your husband might agree with you.'

She put her hands around his neck, the large diamond glinting next to her plain gold band. As soon as she came out of surgery she always put her rings back on. She liked the feel of them on her hand. Loved the security and message that washed over her every time she slid them back onto her finger. Javier had proposed a few weeks after their reunion at his home, with their wedding hastily planned for a few months later in the chapel on the estate. Both of them had wanted to cement their union, with a wedding filled with their friends and colleagues.

'I brought us something to celebrate the moment,' he said.

'You did?'

He reached down and picked up a bottle of Caitlin's favourite organic wine from the vineyard at home, along with two glasses. Neither of them was a fan of champagne.

'How about we toast to the next year? We have holidays to plan. Staff to train. A new flat to buy, and lots to enjoy.'

Caitlin gave him a curious smile. They had agreed the one-bedroom flat she owned in Barcelona was a little small for them and had been viewing properties to find something more suitable.

They had also developed a new plan for those training to be cardiothoracic surgeons, to get them into Theatre earlier, learn all the techniques they needed and give them adequate mentoring and supervision. It was due to be rolled out across Barcelona, Madrid and

Seville at the same time. They had been extremely busy.

Javier looked at her. 'Are you sure you're okay? You look tired. Is the travelling between two bases taking its toll?'

She knew how lucky they were. Javier piloted them between the cities in the space of just over a few hours, leaving the helipad on the roof of St Aelina's and landing in an airport a few kilometres southwest of Madrid. She could go from St Aelina's to a ward in the hospital in Madrid in around three hours. If anyone should be tired it should be him. But then again, he didn't have quite the same additional stresses on the body that she had.

He opened the wine, poured a little into each glass and handed one to her.

She held it up, looking at it, and smiled. 'Sorry.'

He frowned. 'What do you mean?'

'I want to celebrate the anniversary of our meeting again, but I'll have to sit this one out.'

He was still frowning. 'How come?'

Her smile grew wider. 'Doctor's orders.'

It took only a few seconds for him to catch on. 'Really?'

'Really.'

He took her glass, setting them both on the ledge overlooking the city, picked her up and swung her around, letting out a loud whoop.

She laughed, hitting his shoulder as he set her back down.

'When did you find out?'

'About an hour ago. You're right; I was tired and couldn't quite work out why. Then I checked the calendar and nipped along to Obstetrics to nab a test.'

He was shaking his head. 'You've spoken to someone?'

She rolled her eyes. 'Oh, I was caught by Martin Hernández. He said as soon as we want a scan, to go on down.'

Martin Hernández was the obstetrician she'd worked with on the pregnant woman. They'd become friends during the debrief of the incident and he'd attended their wedding.

Javier put his hand on his wife's stomach. 'We'll need to rethink some plans. We have a new Count or Countess on the way.'

Caitlin kissed her husband on the lips. 'And I can't wait to meet them.'

* * * * *